OUT *of* THIS PLACE

OUT *of* THIS PLACE

EMMA CAMERON

CANDLEWICK PRESS

Copyright © 2012 by Anke Seib

All rights reserved. No part of this book may be reproduced,
transmitted, or stored in an information retrieval system
in any form or by any means, graphic, electronic, or
mechanical, including photocopying, taping, and recording,
without prior written permission from the publisher.

First U.S. edition 2013

Library of Congress Catalog Card Number 2012942672
ISBN 978-0-7636-6404-6

BVG 18 17 16 15 14 13
10 9 8 7 6 5 4 3 2 1

Printed in Berryville, VA, U.S.A.

This book was typeset in Garamond.

Candlewick Press
99 Dover Street
Somerville, Massachusetts 02144

visit us at www.candlewick.com

For Peter, Rosalee, and Allan

Luke

· · · · · · ·

CINNAMON RAIN

My Favorite Place

. . . .

A cave on Pebble Beach,

a bike ride from home,

where the sting of salt air

tears away the built-up wondering

of what to do —

on the last day of holidays,

about Casey,

with my life.

Tomorrow,

school will throw a cover

over the last six weeks

and pack it away.

I don't mind.

One more year

and I will be closer

to wherever I'm going.

And

I'll see Casey again.

When I say it like that, it sounds

like it's meant to be special,

and it will be,

except first day back,

by roll call,

I know it'll be like

we never had a holiday,

and I still won't know what's wrong.

And when the day is over,

she'll say, "See you tomorrow, Luke."

It's like nothing will ever change.

A Change

. . . .

Day two.

Science lesson one.

Mr. Chalmers — the new guy.

We line up at the door

like ducks ready to cross the road.

Fig Murphy stops swearing

when he notices the teacher.

"Right, you people.

I want you in alphabetical order,

and when you come into the room,

I will point out your seat."

So we sit

in our allocated spots,

where we will stay

"for the remainder of the year,

unless I tell you otherwise.

Is that understood?"

"Yes, sir."

(But not really.)

I sit between Imran and Jemma

at the back because

we look like we

can be trusted.

Bongo is in front of me —

third row back —

how long will that last?

Casey is at the front,

next to Fig Murphy.

"Perhaps, Mr. Murphy,

you might catch

some of her manners."

From here

I can't even catch her eye.

The Lesson

. . . .

From the front of the lab,
Mr. C. drones on
about the study of fossils.
Bongo is making a peashooter.
He pulls the ink tube
from his pen,
tears scraps of paper
from his workbook,
chews them like gum,
and lines them up
under his pencil case.
Mr. C. writes on the board.
We copy into our books —
except Bongo.
He loads his peashooter,
takes aim,
and hits Casey in the head.

Again.

And again.

But she doesn't feel it

because her hair is so lush.

When the bell rings,

Casey's long black curls

are decorated

like a Christmas tree,

Bongo's page is empty,

and I know all

about paleontology

and peashooting.

Casey

. . . .

Eight years I've known Casey.

It started with a grin

that reached across the room

the day she joined our class.

I remember

her pencil case clutched in her lap,

fingernails disappearing into red vinyl.

Her oh-so-new black shoes,

feet pigeon-toed under the desk.

And peeking out

from her jacket's bulging pocket,

an orange, fat and round.

"She's new," said Mrs. Edmunds.

"Please look after her."

And I have.

As much as I can.

As much as she lets me.

Some days she laughs and jokes

like one of us,

but other times

she's as close as Mars.

She's often late for school,

and I lend her my workbooks

to help her catch up.

She forgets to bring lunch

at least once a week,

so I offer her mine.

After school and on weekends,

she's "too busy" to hang.

Mostly, I can get her to smile.

But some days

I just can't win.

Nicknames

. . . .

"Lead the class in, Mother Duck,"
says Mr. C. to Seb.
Murmurs and smirks:
"Mother Duck."
"Ha-ha-ha."
And Seb turns pink.
"An experiment—" says Mr. C.
"Yes!" says the class.
"In observation," says Mr. C.
We examine fossils and
are told to write down
our observations
so we can classify
each species.
"Continue to observe,"
says Mr. C.,
and he leaves the room.

I observe

an unclassified species:

Bongo.

Using his compass,

he bores a hole

in the side of the cap

of his pen.

He pulls out the ink tube,

chews a three-centimeter piece

off the end,

then jams that

into the hole.

He hooks up his weapon

to the tap at his workbench

and fires away —

an arc of water

streaming

from one side of the room

to the other.

I yell, "Duck!" and

Seb stands,

placing himself

in the line of fire.

He's answered to it.

That's settled:

it must

be his name.

Great Luck

· · · · · · ·

Duck,

under Bongo's bombardment,

flees to Mr. C.'s bench,

rips a paper towel

from the dispenser,

shoves it under the tap,

and flings

the wad

at Bongo:

direct hit to the chest.

Bongo stops spraying.

Everyone peers

from their hiding spots

behind benches and stools

as he peels

the glob

from his shirt

and pelts it at Duck,

who

again

doesn't.

It splatters

across his scalp

like duck poo.

The door flies open.

Mr. C. strides in,

points at Bongo, and says,

"You're to sit

where I can always see you.

Swap seats with Casey."

Winning

· · · · · · ·

Jemma, Duck, and Bongo
cheer from the sidelines.
I've scored a six
against Mersey High,
the private college of cricket elites
who kick our butts
every season.
I scan the boundary
of Kendall Oval.
Casey sits at the north end,
reading.
When Mersey takes up bat,
I bowl like a demon,
take three wickets in all.
Each time
I look north
and see Casey

still reading.

We lose,

as usual,

and pack up.

"Good game."

"Well done."

Pats on the back,

handshakes all round.

Seared by the sun,

we walk back to school,

line up for the bus home.

Casey, who walks,

smiles on her way past

and says,

"Great bowling, Luke."

Great Bowling

· · · · · · ·

February heat—
the worst kind—
slides sweat down our bodies,
and we bake like chickens
under the E Block stairs,
where Year Ten hangs.
Duck slurps from the bubbler.
Bongo creeps up behind,
jams his finger over the spout,
sprays Duck up the nose.
Duck shoots back,
and Bongo retreats.
Soon, they both man a bubbler,
spray each other until soaked,
then open fire
on the rest of us.
We scatter,

take up positions behind the seats,

and defend ourselves,

drink bottles squirting

until they run dry.

Time for the big guns:

grenades appear from schoolbags.

We hurl them across the quad

in a constant splatter

of apples,

tangerines,

and oranges

that rarely find their target.

I polish an apple

(on my crotch),

and Casey cracks up.

Then I bowl a flipper

that ricochets off a bubbler,

spins over the railing,

and lands on the top stair

at the foot

of our principal.

Our Principal

. . . .

Mr. Tink,

aka Stink,

says we

"can not be trusted . . .

are all equally to blame . . .

need to learn about consequences."

So he cancels our first field trip.

We protest:

send him a letter,

put a petition together,

demand he reconsider,

and get no response.

Bongo buttonholes him

in the car park,

only to be told,

"The matter is closed."

Bongo begs,

pleads,

and whines,

then launches into a tirade

of abuse.

Like that's gonna do it.

Stink stalks off

and leaves Bongo

staring at the ground

in the car park.

In the Main Quad

· · · · · · ·

I watch Casey

playing handball,

stretching and lunging

in those jeans.

I'm not the only one.

When the bell rings,

Bongo, Imran, Duck,

and me

perve,

sigh,

and follow her

to English class —

Romeo and Juliet —

before lunch.

!*!#!*!

How come

I always get stuck

next to Jemma?
Why does she sit so close?
And why is this the last lesson
before Friday afternoon sports?

I pass the weekend
trying to remember
the way Casey smells
and spend an eternity in my room
until Bongo
drags me out
to the mall.
We slug down shakes
at a café.
Through the window,
I glimpse a bounce of black curls,
and I hold my breath.
Casey is loading bags
into the back of a station wagon.

In the Car Park

. . . .

I watch Casey
and her dad
finish unloading.
She wheels the cart
back to its bay
while his thick, meaty hands
slam the hatch door,
then fumble with keys.
Casey opens the door
behind the driver's seat,
but he pulls her away,
closes it,
steps forward,
opens his own,
and slides into his seat.
Once he shuts his door,
Casey reopens hers,

climbs into the car,

and belts up.

They pull out of the car park,

pass the café window,

and I notice the passenger

next to the driver.

He doesn't want

Casey beside him.

He wants

his Rottweiler.

More Nicknames

. . . .

Imran, Bongo, and Duck
all get
their driving learner plates
before me,
the big black L
in a yellow square.
They bragged
for days,
ribbed me all term.
I couldn't care less.
I'm at least
a quarter year younger
but eight weeks smarter.
Imran took two goes,
Bongo and Duck four.
I got it
first go.

So

who's a sucker now, boys?

Like a Hollywood star,

I cruise along Cliff Road

in Dad's Monaro,

smug smile spreading,

until

I hear them laugh,

see them point,

and I remember

Dad's license plate:

IMP,

now preceded by the L plate.

By Monday

I have a new nickname—

LIMP Luke.

Can't wait

till I get my provisional plate.

Then I'll be a PIMP.

Trolley Boys

· · · · · · ·

Imran and I are each
saving to buy a car.
We have after-school jobs
collecting shopping trolleys
in the supermarket car park.
Bongo and Duck show up
most afternoons
because they're bored.
We tell them,
"Put your names down."
"What for?" asks Bongo.
"Earn some money," I say.
He and Duck just grin;
they don't need to *earn* money.
They have their ways.
So they hang around
while Imran and I work.

We trolley-race
through the car park,
careful not to scratch cars
or get busted.
One day, Duck swerves
to avoid this old guy,
stacks it big-time,
and lands headfirst
in the blue bin
behind the fruit shop.
Man, does he stink!
Bongo and Imran
cack so hard
they nearly wet themselves.
But my memory of Casey
there with her dad
means
I don't laugh all that much
in that car park.

My Friend Bongo

. . . .

Sometimes he needs me
because there are days
when his world turns to crap.
Like today.
He wagged school
because his stepdad
gave him a pounding.
So after school I go over
to make sure he's okay,
knock on the front door,
and wait.
When nobody answers,
I sneak round to his window.
"Bongo," I whisper as loud as I can.
"Back door's unlocked," he mumbles.
So I open it,
pat the beagle that sits waiting,

pick my way through a mosaic

of pizza boxes on the floor,

and tiptoe past the

pathetic

drunken

tattooed tub of lard

that snores on the sofa.

In Bongo's Room

. . . .

He lies on the bed,

curled in a ball,

scraped knuckles bulging in fists

jammed under his nose.

Above them

I see the shiner —

as if you could miss it —

but it's only when he speaks

that I notice his lips:

swollen and split,

like an overwatered,

overripe tomato.

I don't know what to say.

Not that it matters,

because Bongo just lies there

while I watch the telly

that sits on the floor

in the corner

between his schoolbag

and a pile of grubby clothes.

The sound is turned down,

and the picture is fuzzy.

Every minute

of the lousy ten I stay

is forced.

I get up to leave,

and Bongo,

still curled in a ball,

says,

"Mum's back in rehab.

Now we'll never get Dylan back."

Dylan

· · · · · · ·

Bongo's half brother

had heroin withdrawal

at birth.

He came home

at first

but later went to live with their gran.

Bongo stayed with his mum

because the welfare mob said

he was too old

for his gran to manage.

Three years ago, she died,

and Dylan got shuffled

all over the place

until Welfare

worked things out.

Sometimes

Bongo gets to see him—

when the welfare people

set up a meeting

in the park by the lake.

It's the weekend,

and I go with Bongo.

He sits next to Dylan,

smiles,

and strokes his head.

And the whole time

the welfare lady sits close by,

stone-faced,

despite what Dylan says.

Dylan Says

. . . .

For a welcome present,

his new family

gave him some "inja turtles."

"Inja turtles?"

Bongo smiles, brow raised.

"Yeah," says Dylan, dead serious.

"That's what they're called

'cause that's what they do:

they injure ya.

And do you know what else?

They are descendants

of the dinosaurs,

who got wiped out

by meteorites.

I seen it at the movies.

It was really exciting.

I saw it yesterday

with Ben.

He's my new brother."

Bongo looks puzzled.

"Your new brother?" he murmurs.

"Sure," says Dylan.

Then he pats Bongo's knee

and says, "Hey, matey,

you look wiped out.

If we was at home,

I could make you a nice cup

of comforty tea."

And then the visit is over.

Comfort Tea

· · · · · · ·

After that visit

Bongo starts using

his own brand of comfort tea.

I see it in his room

in a plastic bag

that pokes out

from under his pillow.

He sees

that I notice,

but he doesn't say anything,

so neither do I.

All weekend

I miss going to Pebble Beach

because I hang with Bongo.

We watch telly

without speaking

for most of the time,

until his stepdad tumbles in,

sloshed as a rainstorm.

He sways inside the doorway,

stares at Bongo

through bloodshot slits,

and belches.

I get to my feet,

and he straightens up.

"Sorry, girls.

Didn't realize I'd interrupted

something."

I snatch up Bongo's schoolbag

and say, "No problem.

We were just leaving."

Shudder and Swallow

. . . .

"Where d'ya think
ya goin'?"
He sneers at Bongo,
who sits up.
My insides shudder,
and I swallow.
"He's staying over at mine.
We gotta study."
A leer and a scoff.
"What? Anatomy?"
"Yeah." I fake a smile,
then turn to Bongo,
backpack held open.
"Grab your gear, mate."
Bongo fumbles through
a pile on the floor.
"That's right. Make sure

ya got ya prettiest undies."
The bag shakes in my grasp,
and Bongo jams his shoes
into it.
Arm around Bongo,
I wink at his stepdad
and say, "See ya."
He mutters,
"That'd be right."
Under his foul stare
we shuffle past him,
then make for the front door.
I've got Bongo out this time,
but I can't always save him.

Save Me

. . . .

First term slides away,
cricket season is over,
and the days shrink
like puddles drying up.
I spend the holidays
increasing my bank balance
with the extra work
I get over Easter.
Then we're back in school,
and time grinds away,
marked by twelve bells a day
and the weekly news bulletin —
a love letter from Stink.
Casey is away a lot,
Imran is already studying
for midyear exams,
and Duck says Bongo

hasn't seen Dylan in weeks.
Even Jemma doesn't say much.
It's like everyone is
operating off-line.
Whenever I can,
I visit Pebble Beach,
because school afternoons
will be too short soon
and only weekends
will be long enough.
Exams come and go,
midyear reports are sent home,
and holidays roll around again.
Winter is here.

Midyear Holidays

· · · · · · ·

I spend time at Pebble Beach
even though the water
is too icy for swimming.
The cave is protected
from the southerly winds,
and I light a fire
to buffer the cold.
Imran is with me.
We're not rostered for work,
but that is where
he tells his parents he'll be.
Otherwise they'd expect him
to stay home and study
the whole of the holidays.
We toast sausages on a barbecue fork
that I keep stashed in the cave
and jam them in rolls

we bought on our way.

Clouds thicken overhead.

As drizzle mists the air,

we lick the last of the sausage grease

from our hands and

mull over Year Eleven subject choices.

Then we are silent,

recognizing Casey

walking that Rottweiler

over the rocks in the rain.

I stand,

peer over the top of the cave,

and see her dad's station wagon

waiting in the car park.

When she and the dog

get into the car,

the engine starts.

Once the sound fades,

Imran starts talking again.

Subject Choices

· · · · · · ·

Late term three.

Why do we have to pick so early?

We all do English,

but aside from that,

I'm clueless.

Bongo and Duck say,

"Just pick the easy stuff."

They chose cheaters' math,

art, photography, computer studies,

and industrial tech.

Jemma and Imran

take advanced math,

physics, chemistry, economics,

and legal studies.

I go for computer studies,

ancient and modern history,

physical health and development,

and cultural studies —

no math.

I say to Casey,

"You taking photography and art?"

She shrugs,

says, "I guess."

But by the end of term,

when lists go up,

her name's not down for either.

Instead,

she's in business admin

and hospitality.

I don't understand

until Imran fills me in

on what it's like

to have parents

who decide things for you.

A Field Trip

. . . .

Mr. Chalmers takes us to
rock platforms near Pebble Beach
to study the effects
of erosion.
When I walk with Casey
along the sand after lunch,
I see it for myself.
"You coming to the
movies Saturday night?" I ask.
"Not sure," she says.
She's never sure,
never knows,
never goes.
"How come?" I ask.
She shrugs,
says, "Just not."
It's always the same.

No weekend sports,

days at the beach,

parties or dates.

"What else you doing

this weekend?" I ask.

"Nothing much."

That's her life.

So much

nothing.

I think,

If Casey lived

in another time or place,

she'd be like a fountain —

bubbles reaching everyone around her.

Instead,

she's as still

as a leaf-littered pond,

dark water evaporating,

waiting desperately for rain.

The Rain

. . . .

Sheets of blur gush down,

filling gutters,

blocking drains,

and flooding the main quad.

After school,

the back oval

is the best waterslide

we've ever tried.

Dozens of us

throw ourselves

into a game

of human bowling.

The rules are vague,

but after ten minutes,

we are muddy

and unrecognizable.

That's a good thing,

because Stink appears,

sleeves rolled up

and ready for business.

He hollers and points,

and we scatter,

loping and laughing

out the back gates.

At next morning's assembly,

Stink chastises and rumbles,

then he threatens.

"Another foolish indiscretion

such as this,

and I will be contacting

your parents."

My Parents

• • • • • • •

Most of the time
Dad serves customers
at the auto-parts shop,
and Mum stays home
to look after Granddad.
She makes pies and scones
for Dad and me,
soups, jellies, and custards
for Granddad.
When I come home
from school or the beach,
she makes me a cuppa
and cinnamon toast
to dry up the rain
that sits on my skin.
Her standard greeting,
"Have ya had a good day?"

gets the usual "Yeah."
Sometimes I'll tell her
what's going on,
and she mostly says,
"That's good, love."
But she never asks for more.
When Dad gets home,
he watches the news
and sometimes some sports.
If we talk,
it's about teams
or their players
or maybe the scores.
They're content with that,
but it's not enough for me.
If I didn't know better,
I'd think I was
adopted.

Adoption

. . . .

Bongo's just heard
about Dylan being adopted
by his foster family,
the Hinksons.
He says, "Don't ever wanna see
my stupid mother again.
It's all her fault."
Then he goes off
to buy some leaf
so he can get bombed.
I used to think
the reason he doped up
was to stop himself from sinking
in all the pain.
Now
I think that clouding the pain
is what's making him sink.

There's a fine line

that Bongo walks

every day.

The Hinksons say

they'll let him see Dylan

whenever he wants,

but Bongo asks me,

"Do you think they will?"

And I say,

"Not if you don't wake up to yourself."

Wake-Up Call

. . . .

I ride my bike
up Madigan's Lane
on my way home
from Pebble Beach.
The days are getting longer,
but not as long as I thought,
and I've left it too late.
Dad always says
that at twilight
it's harder to see things
than it is in the dark
under lights.
I know what he means.
The truck whips past me
and pitches me into bushes
at the side of the road.
I lie there, stunned,

heart galloping so hard
I think it'll wear a hole
clear through my chest.
Saliva floods my mouth,
and before I can swallow,
I puke.
I rip off my jacket,
peel away the sweatshirt
that's stuck to my skin,
and use it
to wipe the sweat
from my neck
and the puke
from my face.

Alone

. . . .

By the time I work out

that I haven't broken anything,

and that my jacket's padding

stopped me from being shredded,

I crawl over,

pick up my bike,

and wobble home.

Everything aches.

It's fully dark now,

not a sliver of moon.

I cross to the other side of the road

so I can see what's coming.

Three times I move off the road,

hug the bushes, and wait

until it's safe to step out.

Once I get honked at.

Could be a hello or

could be a blast—

"Get off the road, you idiot."

Who knows?

Either way,

I'm relieved to get home

and hear Mum say those words.

"Have ya had a good day?"

I tell her, "Yeah."

There are some things

I don't want to share.

What Is Shared?

. . . .

Imran won't say
if he's ever been with a girl,
because he says it's not polite
to share that sort of thing
about another person.
We think that means he hasn't.
Jemma won't tell us
what really happened
the day she and Duck
got locked in the art storeroom
last year in term four.
Duck says,
"I don't even remember
getting locked in."
That's his convenient way
of ducking anything
he won't share.

Bongo doesn't say much at all
about anything anymore.
I think he caught that off Casey,
who's barely spoken in weeks
except to answer questions
in as few monotone words
as possible.
I don't tell her how that
makes me want to pry open her mouth
to check if her tongue is still there
or shake her until something spills out.
Instead,
I share my news.

Good News

. . . .

I have been selected
by the state cricket association
to join in a talent program
over the next school holidays.
The whole group seems lifted
by one small success.
The days get longer,
the sun shines warmer,
jackets stay home.
When the holidays roll round,
Imran is talking,
with enthusiasm even,
about studying for yearly exams.
Jemma will join him
in the town library most days,
because she says she needs
to get her marks right up there

before advanced math next year.
Duck says he's going away
to spend time with his cousins
who live down the coast.
And Bongo says he's hoping
to see Dylan heaps.
Casey doesn't have any plans
that I know of,
but she smiles at everyone else's
and wishes me luck
in the program.

Is Talent Enough?

. . . .

Twenty-six guys
from all over the state,
and I was good enough
to be included.
Talent scouts watch
and say sometimes
these are the moments
that provide the big breaks.
During the day
we practice our drills —
catch, throw, field,
bat, and bowl —
until my body hurts.
At night it's theory,
strategies, statistics, and guest speakers
until my head spins.
Some of the guys

know just where they're heading.

When they ask me,

I say, "Not sure yet."

After dissecting the game

until it lies

splintered and bare,

it's crystal:

pro cricket

is not for me.

So what is?

Careers Day

. . . .

The session is opened
with a speech by Stink.
He talks about choices
and whether or not
some of us
should come back next year.
You'd think they'd do this
before we chose next year's subjects.
(Bright sparks.)
Jemma and Imran
are in search of a degree,
so they talk to the people
at the university stand.
Casey, exploring traineeships,
says, "I'll take whatever I can get."
Bongo and Duck
do a lap of the hall,

scab the freebies from every stand.

Loaded with pencils, rulers,

fridge magnets, and drink bottles,

they hang and joke with

the defense-force guys.

I do three laps of the hall,

each one slower

than the one before.

At the end of the session,

I have a single info sheet

scrunched in my pocket.

Trickle Toward November

· · · · · · ·

The year winds down

with the usual hype.

Exams and reports, but mainly

it's all about the formal:

who's wearing what,

who's taking who,

and where we'll have the after-party.

"Down the beach," says Bongo.

"Cops'll move us on," says Duck.

Jemma says,

"My dad wants to have it at my house."

She rolls her eyes, then giggles.

"As if. I've got plans."

She bats her eyes at me and says,

"Rachel's mum might let her have it."

Silence.

"Who's buying the grog?" she asks.

We stare at Duck,

who shrugs and nods at the same time.

Jemma wafts over to Rachel's crowd.

Casey sighs and shakes her head.

"Can you imagine her drunk?"

More silence.

Bongo nudges Duck,

who straight-out laughs.

But it's Imran

who leans over,

pats me on the back,

and says, "Careful, Luke.

She's got plans."

Why Me?

· · · · · · ·

Imran's right.
Jemma jabbers for weeks
about what she'll wear
and how lucky we are
that she's in charge
of seating arrangements.
She asks if I'll take her,
but I say, "It's tricky,
with four blokes
and only two girls
in our group.
We should all just go together."
So we hire a limo,
plan to meet at Jemma's.
Imran and I rent suits
from Imran's cousin
(mates' rates),

but Bongo and Duck

save their money for beer

and decide to borrow something

from Duck's dad's wardrobe.

Casey hasn't said a word.

Jemma insists that

"if we go as a group,

we all need to match."

Due to a lack of response,

Jemma organizes two bow ties

to match her dress

and tells Casey she can do the same

for Bongo and Duck.

The Big Night

· · · · · · ·

Casey cabs it to Jemma's.
I watch her glide up the drive,
holding her dress as she climbs the steps
so she won't catch the hem.
The green fabric shimmers
like the Emerald City.
"Can't wait to see the boys' ties,"
says Imran.
"They're not wearing any,"
says Casey.
Imran and I are bookends,
with matching suits and
lipstick-red bow ties.
Jemma spills onto the veranda
dressed to overkill
in what's barely a dress.
Bongo and Duck

saunter up the drive

in open-collared shirts.

Bongo's is buttercream

under a burgundy jacket,

and Duck's is mauve

under navy plaid.

Jemma's mum makes them stand,

one each side of Casey,

for a photo.

"You look like a rainbow,"

she says. "Now you three."

Jemma squishes

between Imran and me,

puts her hand on my waistband

and her breath in my ear.

Where the hell is that limo?

Inside the Limo

· · · · · · ·

I wish I wasn't here.

Bare legs wedge alongside mine.

Jemma fondles the hem of her dress

with one hand and

fusses over my hair

with the other.

Her breasts press into me.

I stare out the window,

so relieved when the car stops.

But when we pile out,

she latches onto my arm

above the elbow,

pulling herself close to me.

White wads of flesh

bulge over her dress

and massage my tux.

Don't want to spoil her night

or anyone else's,

so I try to relax.

I go along with the "partners" act,

and by the time the after-party starts

at Rachel's place,

I get into the spirit—literally.

This stuff that Duck's brought

tastes of courage.

After a few and then some,

everything's a laugh.

I forget that Casey's not here,

and Jemma takes me outside.

I'm swallowed up

by determined kisses,

and probing fingers

slide into my pants,

then tug and yank.

The spread of hungry legs

and humping sweat.

It's dark

and pretty blurry.

But I remember enough.

Remembering

. . . .

I wake and my
skull pounds from dehydration,
stomach churns with fermentation,
heart sinks, sometimes cringes,
remembering.
Thank Christ school's over.
Won't have to face Jemma
just yet.
At work, Imran reminds me.
Bongo and Duck drop by,
nudge and wink,
call me Super Stud.
Jemma phones my house.
I don't want to hang out,
so I tell her I'm busy.
I escape to Pebble Beach,
run into her on my way home.

Her smile is brave,

but her eyes say,

"Why don't you want me?"

I want them to stop pleading,

so I take her to a café,

say it was special,

I'll always remember it,

I just want to be friends.

We talk about relationships,

agree not to go down that path

unless we're with someone

who's on the same page.

Coffee's finished, and

Jemma's eyes are normal again,

as is everything.

Until I next see Bongo,

who tells me

he can't see Dylan

anymore.

The Waiting Game

. . . .

Australia Day,

3 p.m.,

sweltering hot.

Despite getting knocked back,

even at Christmas,

Bongo gives it one more shot.

He rang Welfare and

the Hinksons a week ago

but still hasn't heard.

He comes over to my house

to pass the time.

Dad, melted to the couch,

watches cricket on the telly

and hopes we'll win it this year.

Granddad, in the dining room,

armed with an umbrella

and wearing a bike helmet,

peeks through the curtains,

watching for aliens.

Mum hovers at the back door,

fans herself with the paper,

waits for the southerly.

And Bongo, on the front step,

waits for an ice age,

because he reckons

the next time he'll see Dylan

will be when Earth freezes over.

Back to School

· · · · · · ·

It's so changed this year.
We're in different classes
and only meet up
at recess and lunch,
if at all.
Jemma and Imran
jam their heads in books,
and Duck defects,
to the cafeteria mostly,
because Bongo's hardly here.
He's either wagging
or in Stink's office,
where he's lectured about
"poor attitude to schoolwork . . .
lack of regular attendance . . .
disruptive behavior when present."
Casey and I

hide out in the library,

read the paper

(our horoscopes and the comics),

do the crossword,

and deface the photos

of Stink

in the community pages.

We search for novels

to write about in English.

It's the only class we're in

together.

Breakdown

. . . .

Together, Casey and I
walk back from the library,
but my nirvana nosedives
when I see Bongo
on the A Block stairs, where
even Year Sevens don't hang.
He's crouched halfway up,
jammed to one side,
trying to disappear
into the wall.
I stop,
unsure.
Casey is suspended
in the same pose as me.
We're mannequins
for a full minute.
Playground sounds

in the quad behind A Block

fade with

each step

Casey takes

up those

stairs.

In one move,

she peels Bongo's shoulder

from the wall, slides her right leg

into the space, and sits on the step

behind him;

her left leg on his other side

completes the straddle.

His head falls forward,

her arms gather him in, and

she lays her face against his hair.

Then I hear

sounds I've never heard before.

Bongo is grieving.

Grief

· · · · · · ·

It's as though Casey's hold
has opened a portal.
Bongo's sobs are hurled out
like paintballs from a skirmish gun
until their force diminishes
into a trickle of sobs
that wind up the exorcism.
School-yard sounds
climb back
up the stairwell.
Bongo slides his hand,
palm up, under Casey's,
then lifts it to his lips.
Without letting go,
he stands.
I notice the squeeze from Casey—
an affirmation I don't understand,

but one that Bongo seems to.

He nods,

releases his grip,

and slips away.

We watch him disappear

past the school gates.

Then I peer at Casey.

I'm puzzled at what they share

and wonder if I should envy it,

until her dead voice chokes me

when she says,

"I'm scared for him, Luke."

Scary

· · · · · · ·

Duck is first to get his P plate

and a car.

No more bus rides.

Bongo's up front, Jemma in back,

between Imran and me.

Through town Duck's a model driver,

but along Madigan's Lane

he takes corners like

he's in a grand prix,

and we're flung about

like beans in a baby's rattle.

Duck whoops and laughs;

the engine revs faster;

Jemma's nails dig into my arm.

We swing

to the wrong side of the road.

When Duck pulls it back, we fishtail,

seem on track, but then drift

in a slow-motion arc.

"Aaaaaarrrgh!"

Brakes skid,

and the car stops

off the road and in the scrub.

Jemma scrambles over me,

tumbles out the door,

and lets fly at Duck—

more swear words

than I've heard in my life.

Bongo cackles like a freak,

and Duck says,

"You're all right, aren't ya?"

Imran and I slam our doors

and walk Jemma home.

Bongo Is Gone

. . . .

No note.

No phone call.

Nothing.

Friday, Stink told him,

"Lunchtime. My office."

Saturday afternoon I go to his place,

and again on Sunday.

The tub of lard says,

"Ain't seen him.

Looks like he's gone,

and about time too.

Good-for-nothin' waste of space."

Monday at school,

Duck says, "Saw him hitching

late Friday night."

Jemma tries his mobile,

gets a recording that says

the phone's switched off.

By the end of term

the number is

no longer connected.

I register him with Missing Persons

and make a call once a week

to see if there's news.

But I have no luck.

Dumb Luck

· · · · · · ·

My hopes
of becoming a PIMP
are shot
when Dad's car
does a head gasket
and isn't worth fixing.
After a year as LIMP Luke,
I should be relieved, but
I'm gutted
because Dad's mate Phil
lends him his car
while he goes overseas.
Lucky Phil.
Dad says I'm lucky
that Phil will let me drive it.
Lucky Luke — get it?
Yeah, Dad, I get it.

What's he know?
Thanks to Phil
and his license plate,
I will now
be called
a POOF.

Better Luck

· · · · · · ·

In the library
Mr. Chalmers saunters over,
hands me a pamphlet
advertising a scholarship
with this place in the city.
"Saw you take their flyer
last careers day.
They've got a new deal.
Think about it."
He strolls away.
I scan the words.
Rewarding career.
They all say that.
People in need.
There're plenty of them.
Making a difference.
Could I?

I read from start
to finish.
A one-year deal.
Put up in a hostel,
course fees covered,
and hands-on work
with people on the streets.
It's my chance.
If I don't check it out,
I'll never know.

The Unknown

· · · · · · ·

The train pulls out,
and I settle in
for the three-hour trip.
It's the first time
I think about
what it would be like
to leave for good.
The train picks up speed,
its rhythm and pull
matching the thrill
that pumps inside me.
Independence,
a strange place,
new experiences,
and people I don't know.
Really living.
I know

I won't miss school
or my job.
I'll make new friends,
and I'm ready
to leave home.
Then I think about
Casey
and realize
she'll be a long way
from the city.

The City

· · · · · · ·

I hunt down the institute
behind Hodder Square:
a brick box of promise.
A woman at the desk
gives me an info kit,
says to call her
if I need help.
Most of the day I listen
to others, older than me,
sharing their backgrounds:
experiences and bits of paper
that I don't have.
They're set on their course
and so sure of themselves.
I walk the city,
through its crush of people
and its smells:

body odor, rotting food,

vomit, and urine.

A cocktail

of oppression and freedom.

I walk farther

and farther,

sometimes left,

sometimes right.

And I am lost.

Found

. . . .

I glance around,

try to pick out a landmark,

and spot Bongo,

slumped near a shop door.

At least . . .

I think it's him.

His hair is as greasy

as a fish-and-chip dinner,

and his clothes look like

they belong to a hobo.

I scoot over

and slide down beside him.

We sit,

backs to the wall.

"It's not so bad," he says.

"There're places you can go,

like shelters and soup kitchens,

get a feed or a shower,

sometimes a bed."

I stay with him so long,

the institute gets the brush off.

Before I catch the train home,

I say, "You remember how

to use a phone, don't ya?"

I give him all my cash.

He pockets it, says,

"I'm getting it together.

It's just taking a while."

On my way home,

I call into the police station,

register him as found.

My Application

· · · · · · ·

Due by the end of May,
to be accompanied by
two letters of support—
one from Mr. Chalmers,
the other from my boss—
and five hundred words
on why I believe
this is for me,
or rather
why I am for it.
I write about
what I think I can offer,
based on how my personality
matches the institute's ideas
of "qualities essential
to supporting people in need."
I also tell them I have a need:

to help people.

And I'm ready.

I get advice from Imran,

who says, "This is good stuff.

I think you might get it."

I'm not sure,

even when the committee

calls me for an interview.

The Interview

. . . .

A force field of four.
Handshakes, smiles, nods,
and we sit around a thick
wooden desk,
the drawbridge to my future.
They scribble on notepads,
the sound of their pens
scratching the judgmental air.
They ask questions,
and I answer.
"Just be yourself,"
Mr. Chalmers had said.
I tell them I feel like
I've been nudged this way,
and people who need help
fill my life,
and that this isn't just about

helping one person,

or even lots of people,

but about where I fit in.

Their scribbling stops.

Maybe I've rambled

and lost them completely.

Then one of them says,

"We have your references,

but we'd like to speak with

your school principal."

My reply is steady.

"Can you give me some time?

He doesn't know my plans, so

I'd like to speak with him first."

Tackling Stink

. . . .

"You've thought this out?"
Stink drums his fingernails
on his desk.
"I have," I say.
He eyeballs me
like a scientist
examining a tissue culture.
"You've been through a lot,
with your mate disappearing,
but you handle yourself well."
He stares out the window
and huffs, then mutters,
"There're some muddled heads
in your year, that's for certain."
"They're not so bad," I say.
"Some people just need
a bit of support."

His eyes dart back to mine, and
his hands fold across the desk.
Leaning forward, he says,
"Perhaps, but I think some
deserve it more than others.
You have mine."
I thank him and slide from my seat.
"So." Stink drums the desk again.
"That leaves one question.
What will you do
if you don't get the scholarship?"

Answers

. . . .

Do I need the scholarship?
If I miss out, will I stay?
At Pebble Beach, in the rain,
I shuffle through the bush
at the fringe of the dunes.
The smell of leaves —
like toasted fruit loaf.
At the edge of some rocks,
I spot Casey, wander over,
and see she is crying.
"You okay?" I ask.
"I can't stand much more, Luke.
I've gotta get out."
With my thumbs
I brush the tears
across her cheeks.
"Some of us will leave soon.

You could get a job.

Maybe share a place."

She pushes my hands away,

and her words splatter the air.

"Not with someone from here.

I want out of this place.

With no reminders."

It stings —

sulfur tears

in cinnamon rain.

Moving On

. . . .

Now that I know

where I stand,

there are no more questions.

But there are things

to take care of.

My boss promises

I will be called first

for registers, packing,

back dock, and stock take.

"At least forty hours a week."

At casual rates

for the next six months,

it's enough

to pay course fees

and board for next year

in case I don't get the scholarship.

There goes my car.

Once in the city,

I'll get part-time work

to pay for extras.

I tell Mum and Dad.

"That's great," says Mum.

"We're real proud," says Dad.

"What's for dinner?" says Granddad.

Last thing left to do

is sign out of school.

Signing Out

· · · · · · ·

It's period four,
a half hour before recess.
My textbooks returned,
I thank Mr. Chalmers
and Mr. Tink,
then drift
through empty corridors
that echo with sounds
of lessons
behind closed doors.
I wait by the bubblers,
squirt some water
up the wall,
and grin.
The bell sounds.
I remember handball,
food fights,

punished pranks,

and I watch kids tumble

from classroom

to playground.

When I tell the others,

Jemma flings herself at me.

"My God, Luke.

You can't leave us."

Imran says he'll see me plenty

when he's wheeling shopping carts

and I'm working my butt off.

Casey says,

"That's fantastic news, Luke."

Then she smiles like it's

the first time she's seen sun

after a decade of winter.

Casey

· · · · · · ·

MY STORY

Who Am I?

. . . .

My name is Casey
but Dad calls me
a case.
Sad case,
basket case,
head case?
Grandma calls me
a love child.
But a love child
should be just that:
born out of love.
Like my sister, Stella, who's
way younger than me.
Seven years is
how long they say
it takes to get the itch
and split.

It took my parents

longer than that

to *want* a child.

I'm just

the reason they married.

Mum says

I was a surprise.

Dad says

I was an accident.

Truth is . . .

I am their mistake.

Mistakes

· · · · · · ·

I know I'm in strife

the second I step

through the door.

It's the way he hollers,

"Casey!"

like his larynx was listening

for my footfall.

"Thought I told you

to get that laundry done."

"I'll do it now."

"It's gonna rain.

Not for nothing I told you

to do it this morning."

"I'm sorry," I mumble.

He huffs.

"So'm I."

Lips suckered,

his breath streams
long and hard
from flared nostrils.
At least his temple vein
isn't pumping.
I put the washing on,
set the table,
chop the veggies —
"not thin enough" —
slice the meat —
"wrong knife,
you've mangled it" —
and I burn the rice.
He forces down
the odd mouthful,
scrapes his leftovers
into the bin,
and I see the vein
pulsing.
Hope Mum gets back soon.

Soon

. . . .

Sixteen years and counting.

Days forever trying.

Nights wasted wondering.

Holed up in my room,

I imagine

being Jemma,

who gets by with

coy giggles

and sunshine smiles,

even though she

doesn't

have all the answers.

Luke learns too much:

when he's not asking questions,

he's searching,

always finding out.

Unlike Duck, who's clueless

or perhaps doesn't care.

Imran cares too much,

does everything

to please his parents,

his destiny already decided.

Bongo's parents —

I snap to;

I'm not that unlucky.

But one day,

soon . . .

I'll walk.

A Walk

. . . .

Pebble Beach,

midwinter,

nonstop drizzle.

I clamber over rocks

with Titan,

our Rottweiler.

I juggle an umbrella

in one hand,

his leash

in the other.

Whenever he sees a gull,

he tugs and strains.

"Knock it off,

stupid dog."

I try to jerk him back,

but it's pointless.

We struggle along the beach,

sand scrubbing my icy feet.

"Go barefoot,"

Dad had said.

"You can wash your feet

before you get back in the car.

Then you can get into

dry socks and shoes.

You'll be warm, then."

Just like him.

Lying back,

snoozing away.

Clean Getaway

. . . .

From the cave

in the rocks,

smoke rises.

Out the corner of my eye,

I spy

Luke and Imran,

backs to the beach,

protecting the fire

while they scorch sausages.

The smell is divine.

Titan slobbers,

lunges toward it

till I wrangle him back,

angle the umbrella

to screen me from the boys.

I run Titan up the beach,

slowing only

once I'm out of their sight.
Even Imran spends holidays
doing what *he* wants.
On my way back,
the umbrella shields me
again.
Dad hands a bottle of water
out the window.
I rinse my feet,
slide into the car,
and sink down in my seat
as Dad drives us home.

Home

· · · · · · ·

We once lived near Grandma.

She visited each day,

filling our world with

card games and woolly knits.

Her click-clacking needles

were fairies tap-dancing,

singing up something special

to keep me warm.

End of day,

Dad's knock-off time,

he and she bickered.

Quiet at first,

it niggled and grew,

chasing away fairies

and warmth.

Mum busied herself

folding laundry, making dinner.

Shouts smothered every

wisp of peace.

"They're only little so long.

You never give any time."

"I spend every minute

doing what's needed.

That's how we have

a roof above us."

"I'm talking about

much more than that.

You need to take

full responsibility."

I hid in my room,

hands clamped over ears.

Grandma would hug me close,

promising she'd come tomorrow.

Dad took up the mantra

"I'll show her

full responsibility."

We moved away.

Away

. . . .

Dad always working,
hardly home.
When he was,
all was hushed.
I didn't understand
split shift,
long shift,
doublers.
For me they meant
"Daddy's sleeping."
"Don't rile your sister."
"Keep the noise down."
I'd play dolls, color,
telly turned so low
I'd sit two feet away.
Stella scribbled
in thick black marker

across half the pages

of my best storybook,

filled with people who ventured

where their hearts took them.

Beautiful worlds beyond mine.

I broke the silence.

Dad flew in.

"What the hell happened?"

"She ruined it!"

I howled.

"Jesus, Case,

thought you were hurt."

I was.

I turned up my volume.

He scanned the pages,

stomped to the bin,

and threw my friends away.

"Keep that up

and I'll take

all your books.

Do the same to them."

Screaming, "No, Dad!"

I rescued my treasure.
Two garbage bags taught me
that his threats
should never
be questioned.

Questions

· · · · · · ·

The sign on our front door—
Shift worker sleeping:
Do not knock—
told Luke I was prisoner.
In the playground,
where Stuck-in-the-Mud
meant the slightest tip
froze me to the spot,
his counter-touch
had the power to free me.
We sometimes still laugh
at jokes no one else gets,
often notice things
others don't see.
He always lets me in line
in the cafeteria, at handball,
even shares his lunch

when I forget mine.
He cloaks me in comfort,
but it's those three words —
"You okay, Casey?" —
I can never answer.
His eyes won't leave mine,
awkwardness smothers,
he learns not to pry.
Growing up changes more
than playground games
and body shapes.
While he does walk close,
his barest of touches
can't set me free.

Gifts

. . . .

Mum's back.
"Grandma's on the mend—
sends her love."
Presents appear.
"Purple!" shouts Stella.
She swings the crocheted cardie
over her shoulders,
buttons the clasp
around her neck,
and flutters about.
Mine is soft as a whisper,
and red,
deep as the blood
that runs from Grandma
to me.
It stretches across my back;
a single button secures it

over my breasts.

"Don't cover much," says Dad.

"It's a bolero," says Mum.

"Shows too much midriff."

"You wear something under it,

Daddy," says Stella.

Which I am right now.

"It's pretty snug."

He pauses.

I wait.

Then he says,

"No wearing it

to school."

School

. . . .

Science lab.

Rows of benches

lined with pairs:

Bunsens and tripods,

crucibles and tongs,

Jemma and Imran,

Luke and me.

Two weeks and I still

don't get chemical equations.

Ask Chalmers for help.

He goes over them

three times.

I shake my head for the first two

and, still clueless,

nod on the third.

Bongo and Duck shrug.

"We don't get 'em either."

Imran and Jemma explain it

like talking textbooks.

Over the crucible,

crushed and burning,

I stare at Luke.

Can't ask him;

his eyes show

my pain's

in his heart.

Heartless

. . . .

Jemma's contribution
to a class discussion
on contraception:
"Imagine being lumbered
with a kid you don't want."
In my seat beside Luke,
I stiffen.
"Some screaming brat," she says,
"hanging from your neck."
Though he isn't looking at me,
I feel his attention.
Jemma continues.
"Having to say *so long*
to all your options,
for something that
should never have happened."
Shame digs its fingers

into every cell.

"It'd be like a splinter

lodged under your fingernail

forever."

Luke turns his stare

on Jemma.

Bongo flicks his head

to catch my eye.

The lunch bell rings,

and he steers me

to the cafeteria

for comfort.

Comfort

. . . .

Pie with sauce,

and talk.

Bongo sucks at the mince.

"What's happening

this weekend?"

I nibble at pastry.

"Gotta visit Grandma."

"Don't sound too stoked."

"I like seeing her," I say.

And I do,

but she and Dad

still

get into awful fights,

usually about me.

It makes my insides feel

like they'll explode.

"I need a break."

"Can't you stay home?"

Bongo's eyebrows cha-cha.

I snort. As if!

Although . . .

He grins.

"There's always a way."

Possibilities:

assignments, study, taking sick.

"You look kinda pasty."

"Well, I do feel a bit queasy.

Now that you mention it."

"Nothin' a couple of fingers

down your throat can't fix."

I urge the weekend to

roll on.

Rolling

. . . .

The ball bobbles
up the field.
So good to run,
chase, and whack it
to a teammate.
Rachel traps it,
passes to Jemma,
who charges around
the opposition.
I barrel for the goals,
dodge a defender.
"I'm here."
She passes it to me.
I trap it, fake left,
weave right,
pull back,
let rip.

It streams past the goalie,

smashes into the backboard.

"Woo-hoo!" shouts Jemma.

Embraced in

Rachel's sweaty arms.

"Brilliant, Casey."

It's one of the few times

I truly belong.

"We're having coffee later.

We'll text you to say where."

"Still can't find my mobile."

I'm tossed from their world

when Jemma says,

"God, Case,

how can you live

without one?"

Without

. . . .

Last Christmas,

I opened Grandma's parcel.

"Every young chicky

needs such a lifeline."

Filling the mobile with numbers,

knowing

I'd never use most.

I liked being part of

that world.

Enough to text

Christmas messages

to Jemma, Rachel, Bongo,

and Luke.

Replies:

Welcome to this century! Jemma.

Merry xmas XOXO Rach.

Merry xmas 2U2 Bongo.

Beaut we can

mayb get 2getha

ova hols Luke

Before New Year

Dad scolded me

for texting back and forth

when I should have been

helping Mum.

He snatched it away,

read, *NYE party.*

Wanna come with me?

Eyes dark, voice steel.

"Who's this Luke, then?"

Squirming under his stare.

"Just a friend."

"What's he want from you?"

Lips dry as dust, I managed,

"Nothing."

"That's all he'll get."

He ruled that I'm too young

for parties, boys, and mobiles.

Phony

· · · · · · ·

Knees knocked,

feet splayed,

I slouch on my bed,

dressed in Sunday best,

rubbing my stomach,

thinking of Bongo.

Mum pops her head in.

"You okay?"

I shrug.

Belch.

Shudder.

Jingling car keys —

Dad striding up the hall.

His thumb signals it's time.

Three steps from the front door

I about-face,

bolt for the bathroom,

slam the door,

flick the toilet seat up,

ram fingers down my throat,

deeper

and deeper,

till my eyes water

and my innards flip.

Tea and toast

hurl and splatter.

The door creaks open.

I cough, gag, and heave.

Porridge flumps out.

Staying In

. . . .

Strings of saliva

bungee over the bowl.

My nose clogs.

Tears well.

"I'm sorry, Mum."

She helps me wash my face.

Dad appears, says,

"Maybe we should stay home."

Stella squeals from the hall,

"No, Daddy."

Mum pats my face dry.

"We can't. Mum needs us."

"Well, I'll stay with Case.

You and Stella can go."

I blow my nose

on some loo paper.

"Scotsdale and back in a day?"

asks Mum, rubbing my back.

"That's too long a drive

for me."

I belch again.

"I'll be fine on my own."

"You sure?" says Mum.

"Yeah. Think I'll go

back to bed."

"Best thing," says Dad.

Mum cleans up the bathroom;

I climb into pj's.

"I'll wait in the car," says Dad.

"Take it easy, Case."

Mum pecks me

on the forehead.

"We'll be back

around eight."

Eight Knocks

. . . .

Less than a minute

after they've gone,

I hear the knocks,

bolt to the bathroom,

race a toothbrush

over my teeth,

swirl some mouthwash.

Again, eight knocks.

"Coming."

The mirror catches

my reflection.

Sylvester chases Tweety Pie

on my pj's.

Sufferin' succotash!

More knocking.

Ten this time.

I squirt Mum's perfume

onto my neck,

let out my ponytail,

tousle my hair,

charge down the hall.

Through the peephole

I see nothing.

It's covered.

I swing the door back,

catching Bongo,

hand still in the air,

finger pointing up.

"Cute jammies." He smirks.

"Shuddup. I'm sick."

Fully Sick

· · · · · · ·

Grilled cheese toasties

and hot chocolate.

"Needed that," I say.

"My gut was empty."

"I'm proud of ya,"

says Bongo.

We nestle on the couch,

watch movies,

chat, laugh,

divulge.

Bongo points at photos

on our sideboard.

"She's cute,

your sister,

hey?"

"Sometimes."

From his wallet

he pulls a picture

of his brother, Dylan.

"He'll be five soon."

"Don't see him much,

do you?"

"Not enough."

He slides Dylan back,

inside his safe place,

clears his throat,

rubs his finger

above his lip,

and sniffs.

The movie winds up,

happy-ever-after music plays,

and we sit,

knees, elbows, arms

touching,

watching credits roll

as darkness settles.

Down to Earth

. . . .

Dad brushes the note aside.
"You know the deal:
daytime excursions are fine;
overnighters are out."
He reads the paper.
"We're studying rain forests."
No reply.
"It's really important."
"Not enough to let
a whole year loose,
alone in the bush."
"Supervised. Teachers go."
"They can't keep
a proper eye on things."
"How am I meant
to learn, then?"
"Don't argue with me."

Still and steady: "I'm not."

"Casey," Mum warns.

His hands clench.

Quietly: "I'm only asking."

Menace in his throat:

"Backchatting."

Swallow. "Sorry.

I wanna . . ."

get out of here

". . . pass the subject."

His whole body stiffens.

"What bloody camping trip

did you miss

that made you fail

chemical equations?"

I drop my head.

"Answer me!" he shouts.

"None," I say.

Down and Out

. . . .

Week six, term three.
Slowest week of my life.
Everyone else is at camp,
except Fig Murphy,
who's banned.
"Mum'll give me
a sick note," he'd told me.
"Why don't you get one?"
So I checked Dad's shift:
he'd be home all day.
My heart slid.
I work in the library,
read,
think about what happens
after Year Ten.
Clock ticks, so slow.
I check out websites.

You don't get paid enough
to leave home
when you're sixteen.
Live with Grandma
Years Eleven and Twelve?
Dad would freak,
maybe drag me back,
make things worse.
Stare at the door.
Chalmers ambles in,
flicks through the *Times*.
"Same old, same old,"
he says.
He drops the paper
back on the desk,
and once he leaves
I read the headline:
Youth Homelessness on the Up.

On the Up

. . . .

I slide the paper over,
scan job ads.
There's one for a lawyer.
That's what Jemma
wants to be.
She has it mapped out,
even teed up next term's
work experience
with some city firm.
Says she'll do it again
Years Eleven and Twelve.
Her theory:
they'll give her
part-time admin work
once she's at uni.
She has options I don't have
and knows what she wants.

I want out.

No idea

how much longer I can last,

or where I'll go.

Wherever I head

I'll need money.

Gotta think smarter.

Part-time work would

give me experience,

help me build a stash so

I'd have dollars.

Any plan needs money.

Admin clashes with school.

Not much retail going here.

Hospitality's the way to go, but

how can I get Dad to be

sweet with that?

Sweet

· · · · · · ·

Monday, recess,
Jemma flits about,
sharing camping-trip photos.
"I'm gonna show Rachel."
She disappears.
The boys stand around
like they're about to give
a poetry recital,
but no one
wants to go first.
Imran hands me
orange fungi
on a strip of bark.
"We studied them . . .
in biology, remember?"
My fingers trace
the rippled edges.

"Thanks, Imran."

Duck tosses me

half a bag of caramels.

"It's all I had left."

"Wow, thanks, Duck."

From between his bus pass

and his library card

Luke pulls

a four-leaf clover

and lays it on my knee.

It's the perfect gift,

but I can't tell him.

"Ta," I mumble.

Bongo presses a pebble

into my palm.

It's brown, flecked green,

like his eyes.

I'm a princess with

four knights

to watch over me.

Being Watchful

. . . .

At dinner, I slide
a note across the table.
"What's that?" asks Dad.
"Gotta pick next year's
subjects," I say.
Mum reads, sighs, mutters,
"I don't understand
the uni entry stuff."
"We've got no money
for uni," says Dad.
Under the table
I cross my fingers.
"So, I should go with
practical stuff, huh?"
Dad shrugs. "S'pose so."
Mum puts the note down.
"Is it what you want?"

I tilt my head,

nod gently.

Inside, I'm cheering.

"I want to be a teacher,"

says Stella. "Does that need uni?"

"Yep," I tell her.

She puts her fork down

and pouts.

"That's years off

for you," says Dad. "We

might be better fixed

by then."

"Good." Stella smiles.

Everyone has

what they want.

Wanting

· · · · · · ·

School holidays.
Dad's at work,
Mum and Stella are
shopping all afternoon,
and Bongo and I
lie on my bed.
I want him
to press his hands
over my shoulders,
draw them down my arms,
cup them over my hips,
pull me toward him.
Stifle me
with his lips.
But
he just lies
next to me.

"I want a house like this,"

he says.

I scoff.

"With rainbow curtains

and pink carpet?"

My room hasn't changed

since I was seven.

"I mean one that's quiet.

Not full of anger."

"You just happen to be here

at the right time," I say.

But I'm wrong.

The worst part

of today is

our timing.

Bad Timing

. . . .

Bongo sits bolt upright.
"That's your old man."
Footsteps shuffle,
and keys clatter—
dropped
on the hall floor.
"Stay here," I whisper.
I slink from my room,
face hot, throat caught.
Dad tosses the keys
across the kitchen table.
"You're early," I say.
"Yeah."
He grabs a glass,
fills it with water
from the tap.
"What's all this?"

Two glasses,

two plates,

one knife.

"Jemma came over.

We had a snack."

Dad guzzles the water.

"Jemma?"

"From school."

I hold my breath.

Cleaning Up

. . . .

I fill the sink.
"Sorry, Dad, I
should've cleaned up."
He plonks his glass down.
"You shouldn't have had
anyone over
when we're out."
"Sorry. I didn't ask her.
She's pushy. I didn't know
what to tell her."
"Try the truth, Case."
That'd be fatal.
He leans on the sink,
temple pulsing.
I swallow,
keep washing.
"It won't happen again," he says.

"Understood?"

"Yes, Dad."

I pull the plug,

wipe my hands,

dry and pack dishes

away—

which is where

I wish he'd go.

Gone

. . . .

Dad sighs
with the weight of me
on his shoulders.
Then he goes
for his afternoon dump.
I scarper to my room.
Bongo is gone.
My window is open,
screen leaning
against the wall
like a good-bye note.
I fix it in place,
only popping the clips
while the loo flushes.
Inside, I'm a mix of
victory and misery.
At dinner, I force food

down—

I won't wave the banner

of indiscretion

by reminding him

I snacked.

In bed, I grip my bloated

yet hollow stomach

and ask,

"How much longer?"

Shorter

· · · · · · ·

Jemma brags,

"I'm wearing a mini

to the formal.

Don't tell Luke.

I wanna surprise him."

She scoots off to see Rachel.

"Don't think *surprise*

is the word," I say.

Bongo grunts.

"Shock'll be more like it."

Duck laughs.

"Yeah, she's a shocker."

Jemma floats back to us.

"I'm buying super-high heels

and having my hair up.

It'll show off my neck

and stuff.

Lotsa bare skin.

What are you wearing, Casey?"

I shrug,

unsure if I'm

even allowed to go.

"My God, Casey.

It's seven weeks away.

You better get moving

before it's too late."

Not Too Late

. . . .

Mum, Stella, and I
visit the thrift shop,
find a single gown to fit.
Stella ripples the fabric,
and it shimmers.
"It's a princess dress."
I wriggle into it.
"I hate green."
Mum zips it up.
"It's a nice cut."
She's right.
Sleeveless, choker neck —
no cleavage,
so Dad can't complain,
but the fitted bodice
hugs my curves.
A draped wrap'll hide that

till I'm out of the house.

Grandma phones.

I talk about the formal.

"Assume you're not able

to go with a boy."

"Assuming one asked.

It's a group of six.

Jemma, me, four boys."

"They'll be lined up

to dance with you.

Nice way to end the year."

"The holidays will be

so boring, though."

"That's why I called.

I'm off work again soon.

Your mother said

you and Stella

can spend January here."

Here and Now

. . . .

I take a practice run,
trying on shoes
Rachel lent me.
Skinny heels,
slick and black.
Hands fixed on hips,
I smile at the mirror,
swish and sway.
Imagine Bongo
holding me close,
not needing questions
to understand me.
When I lie beside him,
everything makes sense.
"Dad's home," calls Stella,
before blurting all.
"What formal?" he asks.

Mum explains, and

he grunts.

"That's a weeknight.

Don't expect us to

pick you up."

Who else could I ask

that Dad would approve of?

"Can I catch a cab?"

"Long as you pay for it."

I chew my lip and nod.

If he thinks he's making it hard,

he'll feel better.

Do I have enough money?

It'll be close.

Close

. . . .

Three days before

the big night,

Dad starts with the questions.

I reassure him.

"It's inside the hall.

All the teachers go.

The dancing happens

after dinner, speeches, and

award presentations.

There won't be much dancing."

On the night,

my makeup is light.

"You look real decent."

Dad sounds relieved.

"I'm thinking," he continues,

"might be best if I drive."

"I already phoned the cab."

"Cancel it," he says.

"Dad!" I mock scold.

"You wouldn't do that.

You always say,

Bloke's gotta make a living."

He looks a tad lost.

"I haven't booked it

for the home trip yet."

His face relaxes.

"Okay. I'll come get you."

I peck his cheek.

"Thanks, Dad."

And the cab toots.

Party Time

· · · · · · ·

From Jemma's, we limo it,

meet our whole year

at the botanic gardens.

Between photos,

hip flasks do the rounds.

I swig my share, and

when Duck opens his hand,

six white pills

stare up,

magnets to my eyes.

Jemma, Imran, and Luke

shake their heads.

I want one

the way a three-year-old

wants to find

the highest step

she can jump from.

Bongo's grip is firm

when he cups my shoulders.

"You don't want that,"

he murmurs.

"Trust me, Casey.

You never wanna

touch it."

Touching

. . . .

After the dinner and speeches,
there is dancing.
Fast, hard, laid-back,
silly, dorky, slow.
We jiggle in groups,
sway in pairs.
I dance with:
the girls —
we strut and sing;
Bongo, palm pressed flat
and fingers firm
on the small of my back;
Imran, grip clammy,
grin glowing under neon;
Duck, off his face,
hands everywhere;
and I'm grateful

when Jemma intercepts

Luke's beeline for me

as they announce

the last dance.

If I let him touch me,

it'd be like opening

a one-way

telepathic tunnel.

Telepathy

. . . .

Christmas Eve:

a phone call.

Mum trembles,

receiver still in hand.

"Grandma's had a stroke."

She lies in the hospital,

limp and docile.

I want to scream,

"That's not my grandma,"

the one who says,

"Who's for poker?"

"Never reveal your hand,"

and

"Don't let the bastards

beat you."

I wish I'd visited last time

instead of slodging about

with Bongo.
When we're alone,
I slide my fingers
into her good hand
and whisper,
"Who'll help me now,
Grandma?"
Her lips don't move,
but her hand squeezes,
and her eyes,
full of fight,
say, "Don't give up, Case.
Play your cards right."

Biding Time

. . . .

By New Year
we're back from Scotsdale.
Grandma's settled
in a home for veggies.
Mum works catch-up shifts.
I watch Stella every day.
Her friend Emily
needs a sitter too.
Dad says, "Bring her here.
It'll give Stella
someone to play with."
Emily's mum,
made of money,
sends us skating,
bowling,
to movies,
to minigolf.

While the girls are

distracted,

I meet up with Bongo.

He hasn't seen Dylan —

not even for Christmas —

and talks about

leaving.

"I wish," I say.

"You will, just

not yet.

It's different for girls."

I huff, "Tell me about it."

"Be careful, Case,"

he says.

"Always be careful."

Careful

. . . .

I begin with the dollars
Grandma smuggled
in my Chrissie parcel,
as if she knew my need.
Then there's the hundred
Emily's mum palmed me,
"Just to say thanks."
When we're back in school,
I score
two hours every afternoon,
Monday to Thursday,
slicing and dicing
for the Chinese takeout place.
I fib a little to Dad.
"Work experience."
"How long for?" he asks.
"Five weeks is forty hours;

that's one week, really."

He nods with the logic of it.

"No pay, though?" he prods.

"If I'm good enough,

they might keep me on.

My teacher says

it's best to keep it up

for when we leave school."

"Makes sense," he says.

My bank balance

grows.

Shrinking

· · · · · · ·

One Friday night
I hear tapping
at my window.
I stare outside:
Bongo, backpack, jacket.
I close my bedroom door,
thrust the window open.
He hands over his phone.
"Won't be needin' this.
But you might."
My voice croaks.
"Where will you be?"
"Anywhere but here."
His shadow disappears, and
my only sounding board
is the floor.
"Be careful," I whisper.

At school, Duck says,

"Saw him hitching north

Friday night."

Jemma rings his mobile

and says, "It's switched off."

I should tell them it's

hidden under my mattress,

but Luke will ask questions

with answers that might hurt

and can't help.

Duck drifts to another group.

Jemma and Imran

burrow into study.

One colored thread

in our tapestry

is missing,

with three more

unraveling.

Luke and I are

constant,

but I'm

beginning to fray.

Keep Weaving

. . . .

I slave, bank, save,
and, term two,
land work
in a supermarket.
Not the one we shop at.
I crap on to Dad: "The teachers say
to broaden our experience."
He presses. "For how long?"
"Weekends, for a month.
Then I'll decide
which job to keep."
Four weeks in,
he's on my case.
"I'm ditching the Chinese."
Library's not open weekends,
so I say I'll be there
every day after school.

"And you'll work every weekend?"

"For now," I say.

"I'll wind back when
my study load builds."

He stops pushing.

For now.

Now

. . . .

Luke's new plan:

apply for a scholarship,

leave school if successful.

If he snags it,

I'll be more alone,

but it won't be too long

till I find my own future.

I wish for things

to be as simple as

when we were children.

One thing is like it used to be:

it's only us two.

Each day, we're in the library,

sharing the paper.

We laugh over comics,

scoff at our horoscopes,

muddle through crosswords.

What differs is

he hovers around me more,

waiting on Sundays

when I finish work,

wanting to walk me home,

saying, "I'll keep out

of your dad's sight."

He doesn't see

how his kindness,

caring, and longing

pen me in.

Boxed In

· · · · · · ·

I'm crushing garlic
when I hear Dad.
"I wanna see my daughter—
NOW!"
The crusher clatters
to the sink.
"I'm sorry, Mrs. Lee."
My chin wobbles, and
I thrust the apron at her.
Dad's hand pushes
into my spine.
"In the car."
Door wrenched open,
slammed,
engine roars.
I'm flung about
through shaky streets

until brakes skid,

the car lurches,

and I flee

into the house.

Mum's in the kitchen.

"What's going on?"

I place myself so she's

between him and me.

"Your daughter's a liar.

Tell your mother."

I spill.

"Why, Casey?" asks Mum.

"She's up to something,"

he says.

I lie. "I'm not.

I just needed more time

to decide which one to keep."

Dad decides for me.

"You'll keep none."

No More

. . . .

Grandma's voice echoes
in my head:
"Don't ever
let the bastards beat you."
I listen,
count the days.
"Yes, Dad . . .
no, Dad . . .
sorry, Dad . . ."
One sports afternoon,
drizzle sends us home
early.
Avoiding even the sight
of our house,
I seek solace
at Pebble Beach.
If I'm home on time,

Dad won't know.

But Luke does, because

he spots me there.

I blurt things out

that I shouldn't:

I hate him.

Hate my life.

Have to get out.

Luke says, "Some of us

will leave soon.

You could get a job.

Maybe share a place."

I wish he'd stop

offering himself up;

it pulls me further down.

"Not with someone from here," I say.

"I want out of this place.

With no reminders."

I've had enough.

Enough

. . . .

Luke's decided:

scholarship or not,

he's moving on.

When he signs out,

my heart lifts.

My turn is now.

I google,

e-mail job applications,

keep below Dad's radar,

never reveal my hand.

A week later,

I leave a note:

Dear Mum,

Don't worry.

I've got a job,

somewhere to stay,

and I'm safe.

Please don't be angry.

Love, Casey.

I don't say good-bye

to anyone else.

This is the start . . .

a life for me.

Living

. . . .

Monday to Friday,

ten till two,

sandwich artist,

industrial café.

Friday to Sunday nights,

Italian trattoria,

waiting tables,

cleaning the kitchen.

Crash in the trailer park.

Dingy and musty,

the trailer cocoons

endless hours of sleep;

I'm still seeking escape,

even though I've left.

Takes me a few weeks

to notice my neighbors.

Mostly builders.

Mornings they're gone

before I appear.

Friday and Saturday nights,

when I get home,

they're out partying.

Sundays, "a few quiet ones."

Smile, nod, wink.

I remember what Bongo said,

about it being different

for girls.

Boys

· · · · · · ·

It's after eleven

when I get home

to the trailer park.

Cans hiss open.

"Hey, love."

Leer, jeer.

"Come join us."

"No, thanks," I say.

"Why not?"

Belch, wink.

"We're a nice bunch.

Aren't we, fellas?"

Drool, stare.

"Yeah," three more say.

Nervous smile.

"Maybe some other time."

In my van, I gather my gear,

scoot back past the pack,

shower bag and towel

on show.

"She's gettin' cleaned up."

Team laughter.

I head for the toilet block.

Once out of sight,

I dash to reception —

CLOSED.

I send a silent thanks

for Bongo's phone.

Call a cab,

catch it to an ATM,

then a motel

across town.

How the Other Half Lives

· · · · · · ·

I calculate that

three weeks in a motel

would trash my stash.

Real-estate agents say,

"Seventeen and no references?

Sorry, can't help you."

I murmur, "Bullshit,"

to tops of heads

already focused on desks.

I'd rather not

ask Trattoria Tony.

Don't want to owe

favors.

Though, soon,

there'll be no choice.

Not going back home.

I roam the trattoria side of town:

brick homes, not fibro,

flower gardens, not bare lawns,

but no satellites for TV either.

People here

garden, read, walk,

play music, dine out—

some in my restaurant.

Like poor Mrs. Maloney.

Mrs. Maloney

. . . .

She finishes dinner,
pays her bill,
and steps outside.
Townies rip past,
toss a firecracker
at her feet.
I hear the thud
as she hits the road.
Tony and I race out.
"Stay with her," he says.
I stroke her good hand
(the other is mangled
under her hip),
and I think of Grandma.
"You'll be fine," I tell her.
The EMT straps her leg
into a splint.

"You together?" he asks.

I don't want her taken

all alone, so I nod,

ride in the ambulance.

From her purse

I get details.

Age: sixty-three

last week.

Address: near the trattoria.

I fill in her forms

at the hospital.

Hospital Visit

. . . .

Information shared.

Mrs. Maloney —

"Call me Patsy" —

moved here two years ago,

works in the city,

and lives alone.

"I'm newer than that,"

I say.

"Work two part-time jobs.

Finding my feet.

Alone too."

Doctor flits in.

"Hand surgery set for tomorrow,

and that leg needs a cast."

I ask, "What can I do?"

"She's so kind,"

Patsy tells the doctor.

I smile.

"I'll check on your place

if you like.

I can collect your mail

and bring it here. Visit."

Her lips wobble.

"I'd like that.

Hope it's no trouble."

"I'm happy to help."

Helping

. . . .

Early morning,

at Patsy's place,

I check that all's well.

Locked up —

even the garage.

I circle the house,

screened by bushes

that edge a sloped yard.

Underneath

the back of the house,

there's a laundry room

with an external door.

I peer in the window:

tiled floor, shower, toilet!

On the line,

washing waves,

damp with night dew.

I could take it in later,

but where to put it?

On my way to the café,

I buy two nighties, a cardie,

and four pairs of undies.

After work, I buy

an apple, banana, and a pear.

At the hospital,

I deliver the mail

and my offerings.

Offering

. . . .

"Casey, I can't
thank you enough."
"I could take your washing in,
but the laundry room's locked."
Six seconds later,
I clutch the key.
"Could I keep this for now?
Do your washing at your place
rather than lug it home?"
"You're a godsend, Casey."
Patsy quivers.
"It's times like this that I realize
how alone I am.
There're colleagues, of course,
and neighbors, but
we kept to ourselves."
She pulls a floral nightie

from the bag I brought.

"My Alistair set up a studio

to build wooden furniture."

Her thumb brushes

the nightie's collar.

"A month

after we moved in,

he died,

right in that studio."

Her voice almost whispers,

"One never knows

how things will pan out."

Panning Out

· · · · · · ·

One last night
in crisp, clean, white
motel sheets.
I buy a roll-up mattress
and lug my gear
to Patsy's.
The studio
is a gigantic room
off the laundry.
Spotless, tiled floor.
Empty except for
timber, tools,
and tragedy.
I hover
in the space where
Alistair's heart failed.
At the hospital,

the doctor asks Patsy,

"Is there someone at home

who can assist

once you're released?"

I offer.

Patsy's head shakes.

"You can't keep running

between jobs, home, and me."

"I need a new place.

Could I lease Alistair's studio?

I can wash, cook, clean,

run errands, easy."

"If you do all that,

I can hardly charge rent."

Where Alistair took

his last breath,

I first relish freedom.

Freedom

· · · · · · ·

Five days later,
Patsy's home.
For six weeks,
before leaving for the café,
I help bathe and dress her.
At day's end, I cook,
wash, wipe, clean up,
put her to bed.
On weekends,
I shop, vacuum, dust,
keep her company
before trattoria shifts.
When her cast comes off,
Patsy visits my room
for the first time.
Her eyes flit from
jug, toaster, bread, and

canned tuna

to the boxes and microwave

on the floor.

"Not very practical," she says.

"Better than what I had."

She's firm.

"You can't keep this up."

I freeze,

gulp,

murmur, "Okay . . .

I'll find somewhere else."

Hands fly to her lips.

"Heavens, no! I meant

we must set you up better."

Way Better

. . . .

I clear the laundry-room cupboard.

Shelves are now for food,

rods for hangers,

drawers for small things,

racks for shoes

(a whole two pairs!).

My possessions swallowed up.

Patsy asks,

"Is that all you have?"

"There's some in storage."

It's not a total lie.

I buy a used fridge,

perch the microwave

on top.

The laundry bench is

for food prep.

Patsy gives me some

plates, mugs, cutlery,

glassware.

I buy a real bed.

Still loads of space.

Enough for a couch,

table, and chairs,

once I save up.

Two nights midweek,

Patsy cooks for us both.

I bring things from Tony's

for our weekend meals.

She accepts token rent,

agrees it's important

that we each have

our privacy.

Sometimes,

when alone,

I think of my family.

Family

· · · · · · ·

I haven't missed
any birthdays
yet.
Black pen flies
across lined paper,
filling a whole page.
News of jobs,
safe accommodation
with *responsible old lady.*
Absolutely no social life!
Everything to reassure,
nothing to cause angst.
No return address, though.
I'll keep writing,
ease their wondering.
Often, I post caramels
to Grandma.

Patsy returns to work.
Every Saturday afternoon,
once she's done her shopping,
she hands me her
weekly train ticket.
Sundays, I relax
around the harbor, where
families frolic
and lovers languish.
Buskers abound:
singers, dancers, jugglers.
But my favorites
are the musicians.

The Musician

. . . .

Dozens are dotted
along the promenade,
but only one who counts.
On cement he sits,
hunched over his guitar,
fingers loving the strings.
The last note quavers.
My heart hovers
in the hum
and his smile.
Green eyes stare
under tousled brown hair.
"My parents said I'd
amount to nothing, but
look." He signals.
"A regular gig,
playing to thousands."

"Who appreciate it," I say,

indicating the guitar case,

lined with a smattering

of silver and gold.

We banter a little.

"Can I buy you

a coffee?"

he asks.

He Says

. . . .

His name is Lucius.
"It means bringer of light."
He's twenty,
makes his living
giving lessons and busking,
shares a house with five others:
one couple at uni,
two dancers,
a writer.
"Sounds crowded," I say.
He shrugs.
"It's affordable.
And the sunroom's mine."
Over three more Sundays,
we mix coffee with
worldviews
and debates about life,

people, money,

and family.

"It's not about blood,"

says Lucius. "It's

about who you share

your life with.

Where you feel

you really belong."

Belonging

. . . .

"October long weekend
means more people
and more money,"
says Lucius.
"I know you work Sundays,
but I'd love
to take you out
if you can get the night off."
Tony's mother, Francesca,
says she'll work in my place.
Lucius busks till six,
then counts his haul.
We start at a pub.
I've tried wine at Tony's,
bourbon and scotch
at the Year Ten formal.
Can't say either

is my thing.

I taste the beer Lucius orders

and shake my head.

"Vodka and orange," he says.

It's okay; I drink two.

Under the table,

his hand finds mine.

"Not your scene, huh?"

"Too many people."

He leads me to a lane

lit by lanterns.

We eat quesadillas

and fajitas.

He drinks sangria,

orders me a margarita.

"You trying to kill me?"

I ask.

"No. Just want you

to take me home."

That's been my plan

all along.

Playing with Comfort

· · · · · · ·

Somewhere between

August and now,

I knew this

was what I wanted.

On one hand, Lucius

keeps his nails long,

and on the other,

they're filed down.

For his playing, he says.

He trickles his nails

across my breasts,

down my stomach,

along my thighs.

His lips, tongue, and

teeth

set upon my neck,

and I crumble.

His other hand
probes and coaxes
until soft sounds surge
from within me.
When he slides inside,
the weight of his body
brings a comfort
I've never known.
I wish the feeling
would never leave.

Leaves

. . . .

I wake to the scent
of Lucius
in my sheets,
in my hair,
on my skin.
I reach over,
feel the warmth
of where he lay.
Outside,
camellia branches
slap the fence —
or was it his footsteps
on the driveway?
Palm fronds
wave at the windows,
and I laze in bed,
relishing

the public holiday,

my freedom, and

last night.

During the week,

I hum as I work,

smile at customers,

especially

the grumpy ones.

By Sunday,

I can't wait

to see him.

Seeing Him

. . . .

He's a little farther
up the promenade
today.
I recognize a tune
and float over,
not noticing the girl
who nestles beside him
until after he spots me.
I've never seen him
with any girl before.
Fishnets disappear into
her sprayed-on miniskirt;
pierced navel peeks out
below a black tube top;
tattooed dolphin leaps
toward her cleavage.
He smiles, fingers

still strumming.
I smile too, but
my eyes flit back
to her.
Sun glints from dozens
of thin metal bangles
as she strokes hair
from his eyes.
His guitar falls silent.
"Who's for coffee?"
he asks.
"I'll get them," I say.
I line up
for the drinks
and watch
her charming him
with coy smiles
and him
basking
in her attentiveness.

Attentive

. . . .

Her name is Tina.
"I'm here to audition
for a play uptown."
I feign interest in
her past, present,
future.
We sip coffee,
absorb the sounds
that waft from his guitar.
"Lucius is a great player,"
says Tina,
squeezing his thigh.
I decide I've lasted
long enough
not to appear put out
but not so long
to be viewed as

hanging out in hope.

When I say I'm off,

Lucius says,

"We're going for drinks

in about an hour,

if you want to join us."

"Gotta work tonight,"

I say.

Which he'd know.

Knowing

. . . .

Sunday's routine remains
the same as before.
For weeks,
without agenda,
I stroll the harbor,
chat a little with Lucius,
who's alone.
No mention of Tina.
I think of him, and
soft waves of nausea
ripple through me —
draining away
when I switch focus.
"You're lookin' pasty,"
Tony keeps saying.
"You okay?"
I sigh.

"Just tired a lot."

Tony's mum, Francesca,

delivering her

weekend batch of pasta,

peers into my face.

"Something's not right.

Tony,

make some chamomile tea."

Me? he mouths.

But he does it anyway.

"Drink plenty, every day,"

says Francesca. "It's good

for the sick stomach. Yes?"

Who'd argue?

Tony serves my tea.

"Welcome to the family."

The warmth

from both of them

grows inside me.

Inside Me

. . . .

I've tried to ignore
the fact that my period
is late.
What's a week in
an often wacky cycle?
We used condoms,
so nothing to
really worry about.
Except the need for
chamomile tea
and the memory
of Francesca's face.
She knows, I tell myself.
I buy a pregnancy test kit
and compare
the strip in my hand
with the picture

on the box.
Two pink lines
confirm everything.
I hear Dad's voice:
"It's not for nothing I
keep my eye on you."
Then I hear Lucius:
"It's not about blood.
It's about who you
share your life with.
Where you feel
you really belong."
Should I tell him?

Telling Him

. . . .

I dawdle to the harbor,
eyes peeled for Lucius
and maybe Tina,
though I've not seen her
since that first time.
Another someone else —
frayed denim shorts,
yellow bikini top
under black tank.
I skulk behind oak trees,
watch her suck his lips
like a leech,
then release, stand,
dust off her butt,
and wander away.
I wait ten minutes,
bumble over.

He plays me a song,

one of Mum's favorites:

"Killing Me Softly."

I wonder if he knows

that he is.

"You're quiet," he says.

"Counting the prams.

Lots of babies today," I say.

"Never noticed."

He shrugs indifference.

"They're not my thing."

Why would I tell him?

My decision

won't be affected

by his thoughts.

Thoughts

· · · · · · ·

I can always tell him
some other time,
yet I know I won't.
I ponder what thoughts
my parents first had
when they found out.
How did they feel?
Did they talk about
getting rid of me?
Were they both
of the same mind?
What plans of theirs
did I
get in the way of?
I won't raise a kid
and let it think
it isn't wanted.

But could I
nurture and love a child
the way I deserved to be?
I can't give a part of me
away to a stranger.
Nor could I kill my baby.
I need some answers,
and I post a letter, not
telling what's happened,
only
that I'll come home
for Christmas.

Christmas Eve

· · · · · · ·

The front door opens.
"It's Casey!" Stella gasps
from behind Mum.
"Didn't you get
my letter?" I ask.
"We never told her,
in case." Mum hugs me,
then leads us to the kitchen.
"She's almost off to bed."
"Can I stay up?"
"Half an hour," says Dad.
Mum makes me a cuppa,
and I hand over gifts.
Dad's is a basket of
biscuits, chocolates, nuts,
wrapped in cellophane
as if to prove

I've nothing to hide.

"Ta," he grunts.

Mum's and Stella's are

wrapped in gold.

"Can I open it now?"

Stella asks.

"Go for it," I say.

She holds the dress

against her body,

flounces around us,

crimson skirt swishing.

"Your turn, Mum," she says.

Mum squirts the perfume

along her wrist and sniffs.

"My favorite. And I'd run out."

Dad's eyes glance off

the bottle and fix on me.

Family Time

. . . .

Dad sips tea,
eyes off Mum's gift,
huffs and sighs a little
while Mum savors
every detail
of my mundane life:
what my jobs are like,
how much I've learned,
my lack of social life.
Stella is sent
to brush her teeth.
"How old's this Tony?"
Dad asks.
"Older than you.
He's got this typical
Italian mama.
She looks out for me."

"And this Patsy?"

"Works for architects."

I tell of the accident,

how I helped afterward.

"Maybe I'll go into

nursing," I say, trapped

by the truth of the lie.

I'm wondering how

I might ask some questions,

but

no time seems right.

Maybe tomorrow.

I offer to tuck Stella in,

then take myself to bed.

Standing Out

· · · · · · ·

Christmas morning,

Stella shrieks,

"Santa's been!"

She tugs at ribbons,

rips at paper,

extracts her treasures.

Mum unwraps one

from Dad.

"Same as Casey gave you,"

Stella marvels. "Twins."

I grimace. "Sorry, Dad."

"It's fine," he says.

"I feel extra spoiled,"

says Mum.

Stella gives them a joint gift:

a family portrait,

framed in gold pasta shells.

"We drew them at school."
In it, she stands
between Mum and Dad,
holding their hands.
In one corner,
there's a lone figure,
which I figure
is me.
I'm the only one
not smiling.

Smiling

· · · · · · ·

"It's lovely," says Mum.
"Real beaut," says Dad.
Along with Stella,
they beam.
My voice light, I say,
"The part in the middle,
just the three of you,
that's how it would have been
if I hadn't come along."
"But you did," says Mum.
She kisses my forehead,
traipses to the kitchen,
Stella on her heels.
"I wasn't planned, though,"
I say to Dad as we
scrunch up wrapping paper
and shove it in a plastic bag.

"Did you ever think about

getting rid of me?"

He stands still,

stares over my head,

and I take the bag from him.

"Did you?" I ask gently.

"We thought about

lots of things," he says.

We're standing so close,

I can hear his breath.

I press on.

"Why did you end up

doing what you did?"

He locks eyes with me.

"We decided it was

the best thing."

The Best Thing

. . . .

"So, would you
have married Mum
anyway?"
"Probably. Just . . .
maybe not that soon."
"Do you ever wonder
what you missed out on?"
He crams the last
of the paper
into the bag.
"I used to, but . . .
it makes no difference.
Life is what it is."
He's right.
All that counts
is what's best
for my baby and me.

Mum and I
prepare lunch
while Dad and Stella
play in the living room.
"I'm pregnant."
A half-peeled spud
slips from Mum's grasp
and bounces into the sink.
She stares at me
for the longest moment.
Then she picks up the spud
and starts peeling again.

Peeling the Layers

· · · · · · ·

"Aren't you gonna
say something?" I ask.
She rinses her hands,
wipes them on a tea towel.
"Don't know where to start.
My head's reeling.
I didn't even know you
had a boyfriend."
"I don't."
Her eyes probe and
her voice shudders.
"Oh, Casey.
Why did you let this happen?"
"Why did you?" I ask.
"That was different.
We had each other."
"But you still ended up

with a kid you didn't want."

"I wanted you," she insists.

"But Dad didn't," I say.

"Not really.

Not then."

Mum starts slicing

the potatoes into cubes.

"He tried, Casey.

He did his best."

Since growing a new life

inside me,

I've thought about

lots of things.

"I know that now."

Mum stares out the window

and after the longest time says,

"Will you tell your father?"

"Not today," I say.

"Later."

Later

. . . .

Huddled inside the
cave's mouth,
I watch families
on Pebble Beach:
kids bouncing
new boogie boards
down whitewash,
parents dozing
under the sun's
stretching rays,
toddlers flicking sand
with Christmas shovels.
My insides jolt—
it's Luke,
strolling the water's edge,
stooping occasionally
to pick up a shell,

brush the sand away, and

tuck it in his pocket.

He gazes in my direction,

stands stock-still

for a moment,

then half raises his hand.

I'm tempted to look away,

but something stops me.

He's different

somehow—

or maybe it's me.

I wave in return.

He jogs over,

skids to his knees,

and says,

"Didn't expect

to see you here."

Together

· · · · · · ·

Luke wriggles in

beside me,

so full of questions.

A bit like Dad,

except,

with Luke's gentleness,

the questions are welcome.

We share six months.

I blab

about work, Patsy,

Tony, Francesca,

ask about his scholarship.

He shakes his head.

"Didn't get it.

Doesn't matter, though.

Scored a traineeship instead.

I'll be moving to the city

come February."
I meet his gaze,
my past need
to look elsewhere
gone.
Still,
I don't mention my baby.
When he asks
if I have anyone special,
I hesitate,
shiver in the shadow
the cave has stretched
over us.

Us

. . . .

"It's getting late."
Knees buckle as I stand.
"Don't do this, Casey."
I falter.
"Don't leave
like that again."
Luke's tone propels
my eyes
to his face.
I don't see
the boy I once knew.
Before me stands
a friend
who cares.
A second chance.
I let down the barrier.
"I do have to go," I say.

I pull my mobile
from my pocket,
key in his number,
make a promise,
breathe relief.
"Merry Christmas,
Luke."
We hug.
"See you in February."

Boxing Day

. . . .

As the train hurls me
back to my real home,
I untangle my thoughts
and write.
Dear Dad,
I'm glad we talked
at Christmas;
thanks for being honest.
There're things I need
to tell you too.
Please don't look for
reasons;
blame never helps.
Like you said,
life is what it is.
I'm having a baby,
on my own.

Don't be worried,

though,

because

I'm not alone.

I pause,

hoping that's true,

think of Patsy, Tony,

Francesca, and Luke,

then write,

Remember

I am happy,

which I know

is what you want most

for your kid.

I sign it,

Love, Case,

tuck it in my backpack,

and vow I'll post it.

Next year.

New Year

· · · · · · ·

Tony hosts a dinner

for all our regulars.

We work the kitchen,

wait tables, pause

to mingle, eat, and drink.

Patsy and Francesca,

in the corner,

heads close together,

glance my way,

faces serious.

When I join them,

they smile —

sympathetic hens

clucking over their chick.

"It's nearly midnight."

Francesca pats my hand.

"What's your New Year wish?"

So much will alter

once my baby comes.

"Only to stay here."

Patsy's face is

a jigsaw of concern.

"Where else would you be?"

Unsure whether to tell,

I say, "Dunno."

"What do you hope for?"

Francesca asks Patsy.

"A change. I'm retiring

in six months."

"Will you travel?"

"Done that.

Time for a grandchild."

My hand drops to my

stomach as I realize

their lines are rehearsed.

"You know, don't you?"

Tony's voice booms,

"Three, two, one . . .

HAPPY NEW YEAR."

Happy

. . . .

"I guessed." Francesca
pulls me close.
Above the clatter of
spoons on glasses
and "Auld Lang Syne,"
Patsy asks, "Is she right?"
No trace of judgment.
I nod, eyes brimming.
"I want you to stay,"
says Patsy.
"Of course she stays,"
says Francesca. "I want to
be a grandmother too.
But my Tony,
he never gives me this."
Suddenly I'm clenched by
the warmest hugs.

Tony bounds over,

tightens the circle.

"Happy New Year."

He stands back,

eyebrows furrowed.

"What gives?"

We tell.

He prances about

like Rocky Balboa.

"I'm gonna be an uncle!"

"Yeah, right," I say.

"Uncle Tony Pepperoni."

Inside, I tell my baby,

"You're really lucky,

you know that?"

There's no looking back.

Looking Forward

· · · · · · ·

Patsy and I make plans.
By February next year,
my baby will be
seven months old.
I can still work for Tony,
attend school part-time
while Patsy plays nana.
I phone Mum every Sunday.
"When will you tell
your father?" she asks.
Letter safely tucked away,
I say, "Soon."
It still doesn't seem
quite real enough,
even though
my tummy pops out
and I no longer need

to drink chamomile tea.

"My mother is knitting,"

says Tony.

"Wants to know, can the

bambina call her Nonna?"

"Sounds great," I reply,

elbow-deep in soap suds.

"You'll never be rid of her,"

he says.

I grin. "That's good."

He huffs, then puts on

his responsible voice.

"You still not gonna tell

the baby's father?"

"No point."

My smile doesn't falter.

"We've got

all the family

we need."

Showing

· · · · · · ·

I amble to the café

where Luke waits,

leaving his seat

when he spots me.

"Hi, Casey."

Even beneath

late summer sun,

his voice warms me.

He glances at my stomach.

Bulging under a

stretched green tube top.

"I know,

it's a shocking look,

but it's just too hot

and I don't care

what people think."

But I know clothes

are not what

he balked at.

"There's so much

to tell you," I say.

He smiles. "So I see."

And I tell

everything.

"I'll be fine.

Don't look so worried."

"Can't help it."

"Seriously . . . for the

first time in my life

I feel really alive."

Alive

· · · · · · ·

Baby wriggles and squirms.
Patsy joins me for the
ultrasound.
Fascinated, we stare,
struggle to recognize
gray, murky shapes as
the radiographer points out
head, hands, and feet.
"The heartbeat is strong.
Do you want to know
the sex?"
I nod.
It's a girl!
Francesca knits pink
cardigans, bonnets, booties.
Patsy buys
jumpsuits and tiny T-shirts and bibs —

white, "For a contrast."
One of my customers
hands over bags of stuff.
"Glad to be rid of it.
There'll be more to come."
Luke and I shop,
sometimes secondhand,
other times new.
Luke presents me
with a car seat.
"So I can take you both
wherever you have to go."
"I don't expect you
to do that," I say.
His words falter,
quick to correct.
"Sorry, I meant . . .
for whoever you need
to drive you about."
For now,
he offers to take me
to see Grandma.

Grandma

· · · · · · ·

Dozing in a chair,

crocheted blanket of every color

draped over her knees,

spidery hands

in her lap.

Again, I think,

That's not my grandma.

It's as though

only part of her remains.

Yet when I crouch before her,

her face and eyes light up.

A shaky hand strokes my hair.

I lay my head on her knee,

whisper,

"Sorry it's been so long."

When I sit up, I ask,

"Have you been getting my parcels?"

Her eyes flit to the candy jar

on her bedside table,

half filled with caramels.

"I've got a surprise."

I stand,

peel open the front

of my jacket,

place her good hand

on my bump.

"I'm naming her after you.

Celia May."

A tear trickles toward

Grandma's chin,

yet there's no sadness,

just a crooked smile.

Smile

· · · · · · ·

Luke and I
head from Grandma's
to Mum and Dad's.
They're expecting me
but Dad still doesn't know,
that I'm expecting.
Sun vanishes
behind the canopy, then
trees blur and shadow
as we chew up the highway.
I yawn, stretch.
Celia kicks and turns,
causing me to shift
in my seat.
Luke's hand
leaves the wheel,
rests on my bulge,

waits.

Nothing.

"I missed it again!
She'll be out and I'll
never have felt it."

I laugh.

"Three months to go.
You're bound to
get lucky sometime."

Lights from houses
along Pebble Beach
guide us home.

"I can stick around,
in case . . .
if you want."

"Thanks," I say. "But
I need to do this
alone."

New World

. . . .

Luke's car engine
fades into the night.
Mum flings open the door,
hugs me tight,
inspects my torso,
hidden under my jacket.
"Stella's in the bath;
your father's in the kitchen."
I sit across the table from him,
slide the letter over.
"What's this?"
"Please read it all
before you say anything."
His eyes flit across the page,
face tightening,
temple pulsing.
"Jesus, Casey.

What the hell?"

I stare, unashamed.

"Like I said, Dad,

I'm happy.

You could be too."

He reads again,

fingers gripping his mouth.

"It's not the end of the world,"

I say. "Happened to you too,

remember?"

Silence.

"And you did okay,"

I add.

He rubs under his nose,

coughs,

swallows.

"You think?" he asks.

I wait

till I'm sure

he's really listening.

Then I say, "Yeah, Dad.

I do."

Bongo

. . . .

FOREVER FORWARD

Decisions

. . . .

We're in school,
where things are certain:
roll call, report cards,
bells and books,
even "chats" with our principal
come around regularly.
Recess, lunchtime,
food fights, handball.
Each year we grow taller,
buy new uniforms,
school shoes if we have to,
and schoolbags when
the holes get so big
that everyone can read
the graffiti on your ruler.
We ramble out the gates,
and Luke asks us,

"What you doing this weekend?"

"Nothing," says Casey.

Same answer as always

because that's what she does

every weekend,

every afternoon,

every minute

spent away from school.

"Dunno," Duck and I say.

Getting stoned,

avoiding everything,

wishing things were different.

"Wanna go to Pebble Beach?"

Luke asks.

Casey shakes her head,

of course.

Duck says, "Maybe."

As usual, I shrug.

But it would beat

hanging at Luke's place

under sympathetic stares

from his old man and mother.

My Mother

· · · · · · ·

Door slaps shut and
she stomps past —
no eye contact and
stuff the "hello,"
even though it's been months.
Off the walls bounces
the rumble of her:
slamming cupboard doors,
rummaging through drawers,
kicking junk across the floor.
She flings herself
into the kitchen, where I'm
scraping together a sandwich,
squished bread struggling
to contain its dying filling —
a lunchtime effigy of me.
She sniffs. "I'm going."

Don't look at her.
She was supposed to
get clean.
Come back home.
Rescue me from that
psycho pseudo father.
Find my brother.
Take us somewhere else to live.
Just the three of us,
the way it always should have been.
"Tell that bastard he'll see
no more of me," she says.
"Tell him yourself," I say.
And it's on.

It's On

. . . .

Her voice fires from
the starting gate.
"Don't smart-mouth me."
I dump my sandwich,
keep my head down,
shove through the back door.
"David, wait!"
I spin around. "What for?
So you can blame me?
I never caused this.
Can't fix it, either."
Guilt, blame, love, hate,
all wrestle in her face.
"I try, David. *Every* day.
Failed the detox. Again."
Her words tremble. "Every time,
I think, *This is it*."

"Me too," I mumble.

She shifts her bag

into her other arm

and slinks past me,

like a dog done wrong.

"What am I supposed to do?"

I call.

She stands by the mailbox

that's never held

a single page from her

all those times she's been away.

She says, "You're old enough

to take care of yourself.

You don't need me."

But I do.

And so did Dylan.

Because of her,

I can never

see my brother.

My Brother

· · · · · · ·

Dylan—

born withdrawn

under a heroin halo,

raised by Grandma till she died,

then tossed like a Frisbee

around the foster-family circuit.

In the end,

Welfare adopts him out.

No more chances

to be our own family.

"Where do I go, then?"

I ask Mum now.

"This is still your home.

Stay here."

And she's on her way.

In three goes

I kick down the mailbox,

use it like a sledgehammer
to wreck the front gate
and help club the crap
clean out of me.
But she doesn't turn around.
By dark, my backpack's loaded,
a fresh-bought bag of hooch
wedged among some clothes.
My wallet is light.
There're people to see.
Can't knock on Casey's
front door; her old man
would go ape.
Through her window,
I pass up my mobile phone.
Can't say where I'm going,
though I would if I knew.
I'd take her with me
if I could.
All I can do is pull away
from her crestfallen face.
It's no way to say good-bye.

Good-bye

. . . .

Luke's and Duck's homes
are both dark, so
I head to the highway
minus my farewell.
I hitch and get lucky.
"You running away?"
An old guy's face,
wrinkled as my jeans,
peers down from the truck,
its motor chugging.
No point fibbing, I guess.
"How can you tell?"
"Backpackers on holiday
always hold up signs."
I climb in while he keeps on.
"The ones without signs
don't bother with backpacks —

short trips, them ones.

So you're off for keeps

but don't know where to."

I grin. "You're good."

"Learn a lot from looking.

So, who hit ya?"

I stiffen. He's *real* good.

The bruise is days old.

"Stepdad," I mumble.

"I'd be off too," he says.

And he tells me about

places to go and

those to stay away from.

His voice fades into

the hum of the motor

till I doze and dream.

Dreams

. . . .

Casey and I
lay side by side
on her bed once,
when she was home alone.
But I never crossed the line.
You don't do that to a mate,
and Luke's one of the best.
He's loved her forever.
I know,
not because he's ever said;
it was the questions he asked,
like he was trying
to join the dots
that she'd rarely let him see.
Whenever he saw her,
he'd straighten his spine,
and when she walked away,

he would dissolve.

She and I talked about leaving—

not together,

though I reckon she would have

if I'd said the word.

I wake,

parked by a highway gas station,

early-morning traffic

streaming by.

The old guy finishes his delivery,

jams a twenty

and a chocolate bar

into my hand.

"Go on with you," he says.

"It's to help you on your way."

Ways

• • • • • • •

There's a bus
headed for the city.
I tally the passengers
who pile out for breakfast.
Reckon there would be
at least eight spare seats.
When they straggle back,
I mingle among them,
amble aboard, and
shuffle to the back.
I hover near the loo
till it's obvious where
spare seats are and
slide into one.
"Just boarded, luvvy?"
Musk-pink lips dance
in her powder-caked face.

Off to spend time with
her great-grandchildren.
She shares photos and
barley sugars.
"This one's Lucy, and
that's our Michael,
her younger brother."
They grin up at me with
Grandma-loves-us eyes.
Memories of Dylan
grip my throat.
Things should have been
so different
from the way they are
now.

Then

. . . .

I'd spend days with Dylan,
wonder why and how Mum
could not be bothered—
like she'd forgotten
she had another kid.
I'd come home from Grandma's
saying, "He can feed himself now,"
and "Dylan can crawl,"
or "He can say *Mum*."
Sometimes she'd smile,
stick the photos I gave her
on the door of the fridge.
I thought she stayed away
to punish herself
or to not confuse him.
She kept saying she'd visit.
Then I wondered:

was Mum avoiding Grandma?

Truth was

she couldn't track time.

Days, weeks, months

merged into each other

like specks of mold

that invade cheese until

there's more green than yellow.

After Grandma died,

Mum promised she'd

fill in the papers,

talk to Welfare,

get him back.

But she lost the forms,

missed meetings,

and screamed at me

when I tried to remind her.

No Home

· · · · · · ·

From across the street,
I feel eyes latch onto me
as we pile from the bus.
I nod good-bye to
the old lady while
her daughter hugs hello,
then I wander away
to find some lunch.
But a girl is on my heels.
"Got two dollars?"
"Nah," I say.
She tugs my shirtsleeve.
"Lost my phone," she says.
Red-rimmed eyes lined with
thick black smudges
swim above a scrawny frame.
"Please?"

She's probably my age

but looks ten years more:

skin like crumpled paper,

creamy-gray teeth.

"I'm broke." I walk on.

But she keeps after me.

"You must have something.

Bus tickets aren't free."

"Never bought one," I mutter.

"Did you sneak on?"

I nod.

"Where do you live?"

I stop and realize.

"Nowhere."

Her bony hand

welds itself

around my left bicep.

"I'm Ellie.

If you're new here,

I can help you."

So I listen.

Listening

· · · · · · ·

"I've got a squat,"
Ellie tells me.
"Not as flash as a shelter,
but no dumb rules either."
She stops, dead still,
tugs me back,
eyes fixed on a bloke
at a sidewalk café.
He wipes sauce off his lips,
dusts crumbs from his fingers,
takes a final swig of coffee.
When he strolls away,
Ellie swoops like a gull and,
midstride,
snatches the remains
of a toasted focaccia,
gulping it down

before we pass the next shop.

Stopped at the corner,

amid a mob of suits,

we wait for the lights to change,

and she turns to me.

"What? Didn't expect me

to share, did you?"

I say, "Just blown out by

how quick I need to be."

Is this anarchy?

Can't be.

There're always rules.

I realize my face has

given me away

when she says,

"Don't think I'm a thief;

it's been paid for."

Paid For

· · · · · · ·

End-of-day shadows sprawl,

and we jump some fences,

slip between shipping containers:

blue, red, green, brown.

"Here." Ellie signals.

In the closeness of

no circulation,

yellow light glows

over a crumpled body.

"That's Griff," says Ellie.

"And over there, that's Liza."

On a bare mattress

in the darkest corner,

clad in black jeans and tank top,

Liza lies on her back,

straight as a syringe.

Ellie assures me that

Liza is cocaine crooked

and her calm won't last.

As if to prove it,

Liza jumps up,

skims around me twice,

then hovers,

close as a bee seducing pollen.

"Cute." She fingers my hair

and circles some more.

Third trip around,

she scrunches my shirt

and pulls me to her.

My eyes flick to Ellie,

who coaxes Liza away,

hugging her when she sobs,

"Six hundred bucks a day."

Inside,

I shudder to think about

the price Liza pays

for her habit.

Habits

. . . .

Around midnight,
Griff wakes and glances
at Ellie and Liza,
dozing in the corner.
"I'm David," I tell him.
"That's Adam's spot," he says.
So I move.
"That's Mitchell's," he says.
Ellie snuffles, glances over,
and pats the mattress.
I rest beside her warmth,
on mildewy fabric
spotted with cigarette burns.
When Mitchell and Adam arrive,
they toss two cola bottles
and three packs of wafers
onto the floor.

Adam slumps beside Griff,

stares at me like

he wants to break my neck.

Mitchell paces for an hour

while he drills me with questions.

"Where ya from?

How'd ya get here?

Where ya going?"

But he's also full of information.

I suck out what I need.

Beside me, Ellie snores

while Liza mutters to herself

and scratches her fingers

until they bleed.

Then Mitchell says,

"You don't belong here.

I know all the shelters.

I'll help you find one

tomorrow."

And I nod,

grateful.

What's Fair?

. . . .

When I think they're all asleep,

I pull mull and papers

from my backpack.

"You been holding out?"

murmurs Liza.

"I don't need it," I say.

"I'll leave it for Mitchell."

Her legs latch around me

and grip like a vise.

"Leave it for me, and

I'll pay you."

I extract myself.

All I see is my mother.

"You gay?" she asks.

"Just being fair," I say.

She slinks back to her corner

and in accusation says,

"Nothing's fair, David."

Exhaustion brings sleep

and dreams of a young Dylan,

eating from bins

and sleeping in alleys.

When I wake,

Ellie is gone.

Liza folds her blanket,

pulls on her shoes.

"Good luck, Fair Boy," she says,

then steps outside.

Griff shovels wafers with one hand,

strokes a sleeping Adam

with the other,

and Mitchell says,

"Let's scope for a shelter."

Shelter

. . . .

Full . . . full . . . full . . .
"Gotta keep at it."
Fifth time lucky.
The guy in charge,
"Pastor Tim"—
skinny, gray, fifty-something—
gives a thumping handshake.
His wife, Clare, is
round all over, with
bulges trapped inside
her neat white blouse
and navy skirt.
She gives me the rules.
"No smoking, drugs, or alcohol.
Food in common rooms only.
Lights out by eleven.
And *absolutely* no visitors—

ever."

Shared kitchen, bathroom,

dining room, and

sixteen shoe boxes,

each holding a bed, one chair,

and three hooks for clothes.

What can't be hung

gets dumped on the floor.

I'm rostered on breakfast dishes,

wonder why the cook

won't do them

until I learn

everyone's a volunteer,

even Pastor Tim and Clare.

Most mornings burst

with introductions

to new faces

who will, for now,

live here.

Living Here

· · · · · · ·

Not too shabby:

clean bed, laundry,

three feeds a day.

Most of the inmates,

way worse off than me,

trip on their addictions

and get booted out.

More bodies come and go.

A few move on to independence.

I keep to myself,

hit the streets for work:

supermarkets, building sites,

parking stations, cafés, hotels.

Yet I know old jeans,

no references, and

the shelter's phone number

on my applications means

they won't give me a shot.

For weeks

I repeat the cycle,

resigned to the same responses.

In the park,

among the tortured sprawl

of the homeless playing house,

I spot Ellie.

She's left the container.

"Some stuff went down, and

I don't feel safe anymore.

Where are you?" she asks.

"Pastor Tim's," I say.

"Why not try there?"

Her face shifts to a mask.

"Can't," she says.

But her lips twist

like she's unsure.

Stupid Me

. . . .

Can't explain it, but
I feel like I owe her.
Maybe it's the shadows
sliding over her eyes,
hinting of a readiness
to give up.
They remind me of Casey.
"Maybe you could help me,"
prods Ellie.
I remember Clare's rules, and
my hesitation is enough.
Expected betrayal
floods Ellie's face,
so I jump in quick,
before the shades fall for good.
"One night. But that's all."
"It's all I need," she says.

After lights-out,
I sneak Ellie in.
Five silent minutes
locked in the bathroom
fixes her breath but
does little to dull
the dry sweat and street dust
as she snuggles into me
on freshly washed sheets.
By morning she's gone,
along with stacks of stuff
from the kitchen.
And stupid me
is caught on camera
letting her in.
You reckon I'd know
never to trust a junkie.
"We need you to leave,"
says Clare. "You've compromised
everyone's personal security."

Security

. . . .

On the street it's a mix
of powder, crystal,
weed, piss, and paste,
each like a dog that
matches its owner except
roles are reversed.
When the weather is dry
and police patrols are low,
I sleep in the parks;
otherwise it's bus shelters,
under bridges, or
crammed in squats.
The night air catches
screams, shouts, fists,
and sobs.
Yet I don't cringe.
I feel safer here

than I ever did at home.

I scavenge,

make my money last.

Soup vans or kitchens,

laundry and shower at

a community shelter—

no overnight beds, but

it's somewhere to go

during the day.

I use their computer and paper

to apply for jobs that

no one will give me.

This can't be

as good as it gets.

It's outside the shelter,

on a low Wednesday,

that I see Luke.

Luke

. . . .

I'm sitting on the ground,
leaning against the wall,
feeding my face,
and grubby after four days
without a shower.
Luke ambles over and
sits beside me.
His worried face
drags answers from me.
I reassure him that I'm okay.
"How're Duck and Casey?" I ask.
"Don't see Duck so much.
Kicks around with Fig
now that you're not there.
But Casey's good. Only got
one class together, but
we're hanging out a bit."

I doubt that means

outside of school, though

while Luke talks,

I wonder.

When he says he's applied

for a welfare scholarship,

I remember the state I'm in.

My shame grows

when he jams money

into my hands and asks,

"You remember how

to use a phone, don't ya?"

I nod and he

strolls away.

Away

. . . .

Cringing with embarrassment,
I stare at the money.
Everything he had on him,
I'm sure.
I shouldn't need someone
like Luke to fix things.
All night I walk the city,
watching those tripped out
on whatever
they've given in to.
There're three reasons
people get away from here:
gone good, gone bad, or
gone dead.
I won't wind up
like my mother.
So why am I still here?

319

Think.

I pine for

Dylan,

Casey,

a job,

a home,

a life.

Think some more.

By first light,

I'm outside another shelter.

At eight the doors open.

Opening Up

· · · · · · ·

"Here're the rules."
Bert, the bald manager,
slides a list
across his desk, then
points up the poky hall
of raw gray concrete blocks.
"Last one on the left."
I thank his shiny scalp,
settle into my confinement—
more bare concrete.
Then I embrace daily routine.
I'm the model boarder:
days in the kitchen,
working solidly though
never finding paid work,
nights retreating
into my room,

head,

and heart.

Weeks spent

dredging the computer

for my future.

Don't need much.

Work, so I can eat,

space to be myself,

time away from people.

Google *exchange for board,*

scroll screen after screen.

Farms, farms, farms.

Finally, I find one

that gives me hope.

Hope

. . . .

Libby McLeod,
marine researcher,
seeks the assistance
of a reliable
volunteer deckhand.

I ask Bert what he thinks.

"I'm guessing you're

no deckhand," he says.

"I could clean a deck," I say.

His laugh roars louder

than a drag-racing V-8.

First time I've

even seen him smile.

"But can you sail?" he asks.

"I could learn."

I guess.

Bert says,

"Volunteers like free holidays.

They never stay long."

Then his voice drops.

"Reliable beats experienced.

She may take you if

she thinks you'll stay awhile.

I'll help you,

as much as I can."

"You've sailed?" I ask.

"Over forty years.

Can't take you on the water,

but I'll bring in some books."

He pats my back

and heads out of the room,

calling over his shoulder,

"I'll bring some tackle,

show you knots."

Knots

. . . .

Libby says I'll do.

Four weeks till I head

too far away

from Dylan and Casey.

I fiddle with ropes or,

as I now call them,

tackle—

square knots, figure eights,

double, half and clove hitches—

till I'm doing them

in my sleep.

The library DVD

Sailing for Dummies

and six books.

Thoughts tangle,

scramble through text.

Rewind, play, pause,

ask Bert what I need to.

A new vocabulary

fills my world:

astern, abeam, come about,

gaff, jib, forestay, transom.

Bert spends spare moments

checking my progress.

He's not as gruff as I thought.

Lively stories, patient explanations.

He'd make a ripper granddad.

Libby and I e-mail,

sharing bits of ourselves.

Ourselves

· · · · · · ·

She has a PhD,
whatever that means,
and sounds straight as
my ex-principal, Stink,
when she writes about
her thesis and dissertation,
whatever they are.
She knows that
I've just turned eighteen,
didn't finish school,
have no family close by.
I hope she's not
too up on herself.
What would she think
if she knew that
I thought *falling off*
meant going overboard,

327

not turning away from

the direction of the wind?

Or worse, that I thought

true wind was something

that came out your rear end,

not anything to do

with sailing.

Duck would love

that expression.

Maybe that's one joke

I won't share with her.

Wonder what she'll think

of me.

Not Gutless

. . . .

I'm on a train north,
puzzling over why,
when sailing,
a line is called a *sheet*
and *make fast* means
"secure a line"—
nothing to do with
the speed you wanna go.
I close my book and
hope,
for Casey's sake,
that her old man's loosened up.
She, Luke, and Duck
would be in class now.
Unless Luke scored
his scholarship, and
so long as Duck

isn't wagging.
He used to rib me
about being
a suck-up
if I beat him in a test,
a dumb arse
when I didn't,
a gutless girl
because,
to avoid hurting Luke,
I never went after Casey.
Imagine if he knew
I was off to stay with
some square scientist.
He'd stir me about
hanging with oldsters.

Worlds Away

. . . .

Cocooned
under promising rain clouds
and the squabble of gulls,
I gawk at megabucks luxury
berthed by floating pontoons.
Above dark, damp piers
and the ocean's lap,
I stroll timber jetties,
aware of the distance
between myself and
my past.
But this salt air
that fills my lungs
keeps me connected
to Pebble Beach.
That's where I told Luke
about Dylan being fostered

after Grandma died.

"I can't see him unless

Mum gets it together,

and that'll never happen."

"We'll work something out,"

said Luke, mind ticking.

"Find a way for you to see him."

"You'll wear your brain out,"

I'd said.

Now I know that's what it takes

to find a way through life's maze.

I ask a fisherman for directions.

He points. "Two piers that way."

At the end of the wharf,

she sits,

her name,

Truth Seeker,

in looping blue letters

along her thirty-foot hull.

For now,

I'll call her

Destiny.

Destiny

· · · · · · ·

Lean, tanned muscles,
thick honeyed hair
worn in dreads
and streaked by sun.
She lounges on deck,
clad in canvas shorts,
laptop open on long legs,
fingers fondling the keys.
I have to lick my lips
four times
before there's enough saliva
for my tongue to work.
"Libby?"
My voice seems
a planet away.
No reaction.
Did I actually say it?

Or is she just so engrossed

in whatever she's doing?

Try again, dude.

This time she hears.

"David."

She stands and signals.

"Welcome aboard."

I clamber on deck

and rock with the yacht.

"So this is a boat, huh?"

She grins — good start.

"Come. I'll show you

where to put your things."

Below, Libby points out

storage shelves, galley,

toilet in a tight cubicle.

She says, "Only use it

if there's no other choice."

I'd laughed when Bert had said,

"Don't crap against the current,

or it'll come back at you."

I subdue my grin as

Libby says the dining nook

will collapse into my bed,

directly in front of

her bed

in the bow.

Bow

· · · · · · ·

"We'll take a quick sail,"
says Libby. "See what
you've learned."
Zipping my life jacket,
I recall that to *luff up*
means to turn
right into the wind,
but every squall and gale
that I dodged back home
seems less of a threat
than facing this test.
If I blow this,
where do I go?
Libby motors us out
to open water, and
we hoist the sails.
Like a dog in training,

I obey every command—

sometimes instantly,

other times

taking a moment

to digest and interpret.

We skim over the sea,

the salt spray stinging

eyes, lips, and skin,

and my fears fall away

like the waves in our wake.

When Libby calls,

"Come about!"

I release the jib,

pull on the opposite sheet,

and duck under the boom,

scrambling starboard

as we turn.

Once I cleat up again,

Libby says,

"You did great, David."

I dip my head in thanks,

glad I learn well.

After Dark

. . . .

We descend into the hull,
scented with citronella.
Libby fixes the last screen
to keep out what bites.
As she stretches to clip
the overhead latch,
her thin white T-shirt
exposes toned abs.
If I was a mosquito,
I'd sink my teeth
into that.
"Most yachts this size
hold a bed in the stern,"
she says.
I focus on her words
instead of her abs,
ribs, and limbs.

"But I use that space
for research."
Shelves on one side
bulge with textbooks,
a laptop, and folders.
The other side holds
a microscope, slides,
and assorted lab gear.
Libby collapses the table
between two bench seats
lining each side of the hull,
and I make up my bed.
Our pillows are separated
by a thin wooden slat
barely one hand high,
and if I reached over it,
I could touch her face.

Touching

· · · · · · ·

In the dark, Libby's breath
whispers of sleep.
We'll be crammed,
closed up in this space,
together,
no one else around,
for *lots* of long nights.
Duck would be green
if he only knew.
She's more real than
any model
in all of his sports mags.
Visions seep into my groin.
I can't sleep now.
Nothing for it;
gotta get rid of that.
I try not to disrupt

the boat's steady rock
as my hand slides,
lower and lower,
down damp bare skin.
I hope that the low grunt
that gushes from me
doesn't wake her.
I hope not to need
to relieve this agony
every night.
Then again, maybe I do.
As my heart resumes
its normal rhythm,
I drift to sleep
counting Libby's breaths.

Breathing

· · · · · · ·

We borrow the breeze
to scuttle between islands,
sprawled adrift
in an endless spread
of dancing jade ripples.
Often, full weeks pass
with no sight of other craft.
Every two weeks,
we make for port.
At the co-op, I pick up
preordered supplies.
After a shave and shower
at the sailing club,
it's straight back out
on the water again.
We feast on fresh food
our first few days at sea.

Then it's back to
porridge, powdered milk,
tinned spag, chickpeas,
and baked beans.
I'd kill for some lettuce.
If I'm good at my job,
we eat freshly caught
prawns or fish.
I even get creative,
experimenting with lentils —
red, yellow, and brown.
But I don't think Libby cares
what I serve up.
So long as I manage
the mundane essentials
that sustain us,
Libby is able
to keep herself buried.

Digging

· · · · · · ·

Libby observes,

investigates,

and makes notes,

while I keep house,

fish, and snorkel,

think of Dylan and Casey,

and read.

Never used to read.

Libby's textbooks are filled

with thousands of life forms

that inhabit our oceans:

anemones, shellfish,

sea mats and mosses,

corals and sponges.

In the evenings she works.

At first, chats are minimal.

We safeguard our small talk.

I ask about her family.

All achievers.

Carefully worded snippets

that I share about mine

make them sound

almost average.

One night I begin digging.

"Where do you stay

when you're not on the boat?"

"With my parents," she says.

"Doesn't that cramp your style?"

Libby laughs. "What's to cramp?"

"Friends. Or . . ." I swallow.

"Maybe boyfriends."

She huffs. "*They*

only complicate things."

I know I've dug too far

when she says,

"Enough about me.

Tell me about yourself."

Both Hiding

. . . .

I don't want to say:
my mother's useless,
my stepdad's a mongrel,
I can never see my brother,
so here I am.
And I won't tell her
that I haven't a clue
about how to move forward.
I've barely admitted that
to myself.
But somewhere in the mix,
I realize that
she's not just running away.
Her life has a focus.
I've got nothing.
Still,
we're both hiding.

I'm puzzled about

how someone like Libby,

who is so educated

and has such a normal family,

can be in the same boat

as me.

Sometimes I catch her

staring at nothing.

It's like something's missing,

and I'm sure I'm right

because all she can talk about

is the sea:

stars,

lilies,

urchins,

and cucumbers.

I come to learn so much

about these echinoderms.

They soon lurk in my dreams,

mimicking my own life's

past creatures.

Creatures

. . . .

I tap a chart on the wall.
"These look soft.
Why are they called
brittle stars?"
"They let go of body parts
under the mildest provocation.
But they mostly regenerate."
"Yeah?"
"Sure. If one is torn in half,
it usually becomes two."
At the sink, I pry open
stubborn oysters
for our dinner.
"Who'd believe that
sea stars eat mollusks?"
asks Libby.
"How?" I wonder.

"They latch their tube feet
onto either side of the shell
and apply
constant pressure."
Libby's head hovers
over her microscope.
"The mollusk gets tired,
can't stay closed
forever."
She changes slides,
keeps looking and talking.
"When the shell opens,
even slightly,
the sea star's stomach
comes out of its mouth
and slips into the gap.
It sucks the mollusk
right out of its shell."
My own steady pressure
forces open
the last oyster.
Never again

will I let anyone

wear me down like that.

I serve up our meal.

"Come on, Libby.

Time for a break."

Breaking

. . . .

One night

we lie on my bed.

I spill about my mum and

why I can't see Dylan.

Libby speaks of Carl,

from Norway.

"We made lifelong plans.

He went back,

never returned my calls

or e-mails."

She stares outside,

into darkness.

"My brother works in Europe.

He looked Carl up.

He's seeing our plans through

with someone else."

For a while

the only sound

is the ocean

lapping against the hull.

"So you spent ages

wondering

if you'd see him again."

She nods.

More silence

till my voice cuts through.

"I miss my brother like

the sea would miss salt

if that were taken away."

The cabin's air warms.

Libby reaches out,

grips my T-shirt,

pulls herself close,

searches my face.

Her thumb strokes

the back of my hand

where it rests on my ribs.

Her head dips down

past my chest, and

she kisses my fingers.
We find comfort and pleasure
over and again.
Our wanting
never seems to stop.

Wanting

· · · · · · ·

Our throbbing, licking,
fondling, and thrusting
is as routine as our
waking, eating,
working, and sleeping.
Lib still researches with
her old constant drive,
and I perform my role
like a faithful servant.
Sick of tinned tomatoes,
dehydrated peas and beans,
we dock in the harbor.
"I'd kill for a steak.
Can we eat out, Lib?"
Shave, shower, then shop
and pick up her mail.
I spot a black cap

and red T-shirt,

both with leaping dolphins.

"Might post one to Dylan,

maybe for Christmas."

"Grab it now," says Lib.

But my wallet's too thin.

Libby picks up both and

pays for them and dinner.

Once I deliver

my day's final duty,

she quickly falls asleep.

I wonder if the personal costs

of the services I render

might be too dear.

Dear Dylan

. . . .

I mail Dylan's gift.
Don't have an address,
so I have to send it
via his school.
Means it won't get to him
till after Christmas break.
I enclose two notes.
Dear Mr. and Mrs. Hinkson,
I know that you thought
my past behavior
meant it was best
for Dylan to have
no contact with me.
My life has changed a lot,
and for now, what I ask is
that you pass on this gift
so Dylan knows

he's still my brother.
Dear Dylan,
I think of you every day
and miss you heaps.
I hope the Hinksons
let you eat peanut butter
straight from the jar
like I used to let you.
Always try your hardest
at everything you do.
Catch you later, buddy.
David.

I give no return address.
I'd rather just assume
the Hinksons pass it on
than risk the parcel
being sent back.
I'll let them know more
one day.

Scrubbed Out

. . . .

"Gotta earn some dough,"
I tell Libby.
Each week, we spend
two days in the harbor,
me working the co-op.
"Hey," says Thomo,
who's scaling snapper.
"You been round awhile.
Live on *Truth Seeker*
with that research chick.
Don't ya?"
I slice head to tail,
give a light nod,
slop guts into a bucket,
toss the fish on the sink.
"So tell the truth then.
She a bit of all right?"

He's almost drooling.

"She'd be good.

Real good,

I reckon."

It's the same every day —

he never lets up.

"Think I ain't worked out

why you don't shave no more?"

He scrapes,

pauses,

grins,

scrapes some more.

"So you can scrub her

all over,

I reckon."

I tune out

and keep working.

No wonder

he's the one bloke here

without someone

waiting at home,

I reckon.

Making Plans

. . . .

I decide it's time
to head back south,
closer to Dylan.
Like a receding tide,
normal routine pulls away.
I hit the community college.
Days fill with new faces
training alongside me.
Bar skills,
and coffee art.
We carefully steam milk,
avoid scalding ourselves.
Gently tease out
leaves, stars, florals,
while chatting away.
Trent,
bricklayer by day:

"Second baby coming soon;
need another job
while the wife's off work."
Ella, twenty-three,
uni done, travel plans:
"Flowers are tricky.
Not like hearts."
"Hearts can be tricky too,"
says Garry,
divorced, laid off,
no idea what he'll do now.
Back on the boat,
I'm surrounded by
the ebb and flow of
comfortable caring.
"Stewart's still in Europe.
He's happy for you to
keep an eye on his flat."
Libby snuggles beside me,
warm and still.
We decide for my last day
we'll do something special.

Special

. . . .

A hot-air balloon ride
over the hinterlands.
In the predawn darkness
six excited tourists,
us,
and our pilot
board a minibus.
Through the darkness,
we head for a soccer oval,
share reasons for ascending
into the heavens.
"Celebrating graduation."
"Twenty-first birthday."
"Tenth wedding anniversary."
Libby says, "He's leaving me."
Confused faces stare back.
Leaning up against each other,

we laugh, then become still,

meld together.

Everyone lifts

the basket to the ground,

unfolds the silk,

holding it open while it fills.

It hovers upright,

a rainbow of color.

Squeezed inside the basket,

we watch the world fall away,

and everything miniaturizes.

From way up here,

there're no threats,

no obstacles.

I lean up behind Libby,

one arm circling her waist,

the other on the basket's rim.

She places her hand over mine,

fingers warm, thumb stroking.

There are some things

about this way of life

I'll really miss.

Leaving

· · · · · · ·

I watch my last sunrise
alone on the deck.
It reminds me of
Pebble Beach.
Backpack by my feet,
I sit at the foot of my bed,
where Libby still sleeps.
Her nakedness is cloaked
by a draped red sheet.
She wakes
and hands me a tiny
coral brittle star.
"Remember,
even a half
can become whole again."
I pocket the gift,
squeeze the bulge that is

her feet under the sheets,
push myself from the bed,
and without looking back,
clamber up the steps.
My footfalls on the jetty
smack out a rhythm
all the way to the bus.
Twenty minutes later,
it dumps me at the station.
I shuffle aboard a train,
curl up at the end
of the last car,
thinking about
the different sorts of love.

Love

· · · · · · ·

It sure is blind,
or at the very least
stark-raving drunk.
From where I stand,
sober behind the bar,
I watch the city's sad
hunting down every
pale glimpse of affection,
grasping for partners on
the thumping dance floor,
hoping the gyrating grind
of dolled-up, sweated-out,
craving bodies
will answer their prayers.
Night after night,
I'm threatened with cleavage.
It's always the same.

"I've got a thing

for fellas with long hair."

"What'll it be?" I ask.

They yell over the music,

"You'll do."

"It's against the rules,"

I shout. "Sorry."

If they weren't so drunk,

they could tell I'm not.

I half hear, half lip-read,

"Everyone does it.

No one cares."

Mostly

I shake my head,

relenting only

sometimes.

Sometimes

· · · · · · ·

They wait out back,
stumble home with me,
some shyly asking
polite nothings
in unsteady voices.
"Lived here long?"
"Like it?"
"Where you from?"
Others babble about
themselves,
where they go out,
which places are best.
Reserved or quiet ones
usually deliver
morning questions.
"Got any plans today?"
"Leave you my number?"

My brief reply: "Sure."
Not offering mine
is well translated—
they leave.
Others disappear
before I wake.
Beats the awkwardness
of me making busy
while they dress.
Worse is when
sober daylight lifts the shades,
revealing in their eyes
the fact that I'm not wanted.
I know they
won't miss me.

Missing

· · · · · · ·

The train hurtles me back
to my past.
Has anyone missed me?
Imran and Jemma
won't have lifted heads
out of their books.
Duck'll be hanging with
Fig Murphy, I bet.
On daily detention,
probably suspended
at least once by now.
Luke, always there,
still hopeful for Casey,
unless something's changed.
Has he learned what it takes
to make her really smile?
Does she ever

think of me?

Wonder if I can see Dylan.

He deserved a better chance.

They can't hurt him

anymore.

Hope he hasn't

forgotten me.

At two thirty,

I wait across the road

from Dylan's school.

When I spot him

tumbling past the gate,

I want to bolt over, but

my feet stay anchored.

Anchored

· · · · · · ·

Dylan's schoolbag jiggles
up and down on his back
as he races another boy
along the footpath.
They jostle and weave,
then throw themselves
at Mrs. Hinkson.
"I win!" whoops Dylan.
I'm unsure if the other kid
is hers or adopted too.
She hugs them both
like she hasn't seen them
for weeks.
They squirm free,
throw off backpacks,
and charge down the road.
They tug at the door handles

on a new station wagon.

"Is today tae kwon do?"

Dylan yells.

"Yes,"

calls a smiling Mrs. Hinkson,

struggling to keep up.

Zap. Doors unlock.

She loads their bags in the back,

and the boys buckle up.

I stay hidden behind my beard.

When I see Dylan put on

the cap I sent,

the ache of absence

recedes.

The portal will be there

when it's time

to cross through.

For now it's enough

to know he's settled

and safe.

Unsettling

· · · · · · ·

At one end of the high school,

weighed down with books,

Jemma and Imran stroll

through the car park

to a dented old hatchback.

"Finally got yourself a

dream machine?"

I chuckle as Imran

unlocks the driver's door.

He gives a confused stare

that turns to pleased recognition

as Jemma gasps, "Bongo."

"D'ya miss me?" I ask.

The reply: a light

friendly jab to my arm.

"What have you been up to?

What brings you back?"

"Wanted to check out

how everyone's doing."

Jemma stays silent,

so unlike her.

Her eyes flit back

to Imran

every two seconds.

Something is wrong.

"Luke's left school.

Got a traineeship,"

says Imran.

Jemma clenches her hands,

stares at her fingernails.

Wish she'd cut that out.

"What about Duck?" I ask.

"You don't know?"

I'm chilled by Imran's voice,

duller than I've ever heard it.

"He's dead."

I shake my head.

They're just words.

They mean nothing.

Imran's mouth keeps moving.

"He was driving one night . . .

lost control."

"Nah," I say.

That can't be right.

So Wrong

. . . .

Outside Duck's house

between weeds and vines,

violets that carpet the yard

no longer dance,

their drooped heads

too dull to nod.

Glossy green leaves gone,

the overgrown bushes

splay curled claws

before draped windows.

Clouds converge overhead,

dull gray, darkening.

A rumble escorts me

to the memorial gardens.

First blotches of rain

hit cold and thick as

I spot the plaque.

The truth stares me down.

Sebastian Carrick

Always smiling,

forever missed.

The only thing left

to prove he ever was.

Raindrops increase

in number and speed,

pummeling so hard,

bouncing off the ground,

drenching me down.

Down

. . . .

Hours later,
clothes still sopping,
I crack open my first beer
inside the flat I'm minding.
I drench my insides
and, shivering, I shower,
hot spray stinging
as the news really seeps in.
Suck down a second,
pungent yeast and hops
reminding me of Duck
swiping his old man's.
"Can't afford this brand."
I smile at the memory,
the reason I chose it.
Sink into the couch,
flick on the telly,

pick at pizza.

Drink to and for Duck,

dill-brain who was

scared of cockroaches,

thought test-tube babies

would mean the end of sex,

and never noticed

if he had his shoes

on the wrong feet.

More beer.

Remember cracking up

when he spun off the road

and Jemma spat it big-time.

I needed laughs then,

not a dead idiot mate now.

Beer number six,

more than pissed off

about his useless driving.

Keep drinking.

Burrow into the couch,

face wet, tears sneaking out.

The telly is invaded

by hallelujah channels

and infomercials,

both trying to sell

everything needed

to save you.

Saved

. . . .

Bert grins as if
something he's wanted
has fallen into place.
I've offered to help out
every Tuesday,
because I can.
"We never knock back
willing hands," he says.
Faces change,
though stories, needs,
and failed ambitions
don't.
A fourteen-year-old upstart:
"Not washing up.
Never ate here all day."
Today's cook says, "You sleep here.
Use the facilities."

I tap the roster. "Your turn."

"Can't boss me around."

He kicks out, toppling bins,

shatters crockery to the floor,

snatches up a knife.

I step slowly, carefully,

around plate shards,

stand sentry,

signal the cook to back away.

The kid lunges. I boot

into his gut,

send him sprawling.

Knife flings skyward;

cook pounces on it.

I pin the turd down,

grunt, "Have to do better.

I've had lotsa practice."

Security arrives

and takes him away.

The cook dabs disinfectant

over my sliced shin.

"Tomorrow will be nicer."

Some Certainties

. . . .

In Bert's office
I stare at pinned-up photos
of people who've stayed here,
photos taken once back on track
and right before leaving.
Bright, hopeful, smiling.
Can't ever be certain
how many make it.
Some return for help —
which beats those that don't
even though they need it.
Pictures of anyone
whose name we find
in a newspaper obituary
are always taken down
and filed away
with the death notice.

They now live only
in Bert's archives.
I open my wallet and
smile at my brother,
certain he'll never appear
on a wall like this.
And I know
this won't be
my last photo of him.
Staring back through the faces,
I wonder how many found
what they were looking for
and how many
are still searching.

Searching

· · · · · · ·

I long to twine up
with somebody.
Not from the nightclubs.
The pier's gift-shop girl, Aimee,
always smiling,
helping me find presents.
"Perfect for your brother."
A crowded café,
as end-of-day waitstaff
swap with the dinner crew.
One winks at Aimee
and, leaving, says, "Have fun."
Beautiful, sweet, lovely
Aimee.
I feign interest
when a twenty-question quiz
showers down:

birth date,

middle name,

favorite color,

dream car,

best holiday.

It's a game Casey and I

never needed to play.

A waitress appears.

"Staying for dinner?"

"Sorry, gotta bolt," I say.

I give Aimee my number—

rude not to, after coffee.

Manners can disappear later

when I ignore calls.

Shouldn't have to try

so hard.

The true test is won

when being together

without saying a word

is everything.

The Only One

. . . .

August winds trap me
in Libby's brother's flat.
Outside the window
a pigeon nests,
calling for its mate.
Rhythm, soft and comforting,
building steadily,
singing its need.
No answer.
It keeps calling.
Pleading, begging, hoping.
Casey's image —
ebony curls, perfect feet,
tiny hands —
reaches for me.
I know her,
felt her hope

when she lay with me.

A distant reply,

promising return.

Flutter of wings

and stillness

once the pigeon's mate lands,

settling in

to the space

they share.

Luke's left Pebble Beach.

Probably worked out that

she doesn't long for him.

Soon, school will be done,

Casey will be free

to find someone else,

and I'll wind up

without.

Her old man

can't rule forever.

I need to ask

the question.

Answers

. . . .

"Where's Casey?" I ask.

"She's not here," says Stella.

"Luke took her and the baby

back home yesterday."

I balk.

"The baby? Luke . . . and

Casey and the baby?"

"Mmm." Stella nods.

I nod in return

because no words come.

On numb, heavy legs

I back down the drive

and take a dazed trip

to the train station.

The whole ride home, I rock.

Only some of that's

from the train's momentum.

I left it too late.

Way too late.

Couldn't take her with me

back then.

Couldn't have given her

what she needed.

Over and over

I punch the train wall.

Every Sunday passenger

slinks to another car.

I'm all alone,

fuming at myself,

waving a great flag

of failure.

Choices

. . . .

In the shelter kitchen
I slam a box on the sink.
Tahlia, sixteen,
peeling spuds,
flinches.
I rip at the cardboard,
yank open the freezer door,
smack in plastic packs
of prefrozen rissoles.
Tahlia drops everything
and flees to her room.
I finish the spuds off,
stop grinding my teeth.
Wasn't her fault.
I stay for dinner,
apologize.
"I scare easy," she says.

Her father was a monster.

She tells me

she can't understand

what she did

to make him

treat her that way.

"Nothing," I say.

"I'm not going back."

"You don't have to," I say.

She pushes her plate away,

rests her head

on the table.

"But I want to.

I miss my friends."

Friends

. . . .

Won't risk losing
anyone else
special to me.
"Luke, it's David."
"David? Which . . .
oh, Bongo!"
"I dropped in to see you.
Heard the three of you
were up here now.
How is everyone?"
"We're all good.
Casey and Celia are great."
Swallow hard.
"I'd like to catch up," I say.
"We'd love that."
Arrangements are made.
Once ready, I stare

into the mirror.

No beard or head of hair

can hide every feeling.

Hope I'm gutsy enough,

friend enough,

to let my past wish

disappear

once I see them

together.

I pocket the starfish

Libby gave me,

clutch it on the train,

and all the way down

the driveway to their door,

keeping hold of the thought

that a half can become

whole again.

I want them in my life.

Introductions

· · · · · · ·

Jiggling

a crocheted pink bundle

in her arms,

Casey opens the door.

She looks different.

Same long black curls

and slender body, but

she's relaxed and bright,

not guarded and still.

"What's with the beard?"

"You like it?" I ask.

"Mmm. And the hair."

Okay, no flirting.

She's Luke's.

Mother of his kid.

Still,

it slips out.

"Nice baby," I quip.

Stop it.

Smarten up.

I shake Luke's hand.

Casey sits,

pats the couch, and

I sit

beside her,

though not too close.

She introduces Celia.

Plump, round, and

glowing.

I remember Dylan.

Frail, gray, tiny.

Celia gurgles softly.

Casey kisses her forehead,

then stands.

"I'll scoot to the trattoria

for coffee and cake."

Luke offers to go.

"I need the walk," she says.

As she rests Celia

in my lap,

she asks,

"Can I trust you?"

I answer,

"Always."

Fathers

. . . .

Luke sits across from me.

"Casey looks happy," I say.

"Especially now that you're here,"

he answers. "You always

could make her laugh."

"You must be

doing something right."

He shrugs. "Same as always."

I wince as Celia tugs my hair.

"Gotta watch that," Luke says.

He peels her fingers away

and she whines.

When he picks her up,

she hushes.

"How's it feel being a family?"

"She's not mine."

"Oh . . .

have you met him?"

"He's not part of their lives.

Casey says she'll never

tell him about Celia."

Two things Celia and I share:

a birth certificate

that says *father unknown* and

a stepdad.

"You'll be perfect, Luke."

"Not just Celia," he says.

"Neither of them is mine."

He sits, holding Celia close.

"I just assumed," I say.

"Strange, isn't it?" he asks.

"Where life takes you and

how much can change."

Looking Forward

. . . .

Celia lies on her back
on a fluffy white rug,
legs kicking,
arms waving.
"Backstroke," says Luke.
"Bath time," decides Casey.
I comment that the stench
of used nappies is deadly.
"Get used to it," says Luke,
preparing a fresh one.
While Celia splashes Casey,
I bag and dump the full nappy
straight into the bin outside.
We plan places to take her:
zoo, harbor, aquarium.
Casey feeds then swaddles her,
settles her into bed.

Music box plays while

we hover over the crib,

whispering.

"Reckon she'll play cricket?"

asks Luke.

"Hockey," answers Casey.

I'll take her sailing

with Dylan.

We compare schedules

and plan a picnic

for next week.

So much

to look forward to.

Author's Note

I am fascinated by watching people finding their way in life. I delight in their resilience, resourcefulness, and ability to continue seeking what they feel is best for them. I'm often amazed at how uncertainty has the power to prevent someone from moving forward and how what is unspoken may sometimes have a greater influence on people than what is said. Still, I always hope that where people end up is not too far away from where they had aimed to be. It's nice to think that picking uncertain paths may not necessarily alter one's destination too drastically, simply the journey undertaken to reach it.

Initially the characters in *Out of This Place* came to me through Luke (who nagged me to write their story). Once I began, I enjoyed watching him, Casey, and David grow as they made choices and took the paths they felt they needed to. I was also delighted to see that their choices brought them together again, as I felt they were destined to share more of their lives than only what is told in this story.

Acknowledgments

My thanks to Vicki Stanton, Sandi Wooton, Kathryn Edmonds, and Lilli Rodrigues-Pang for embarking on the writing journey with me and for always being there.

I am grateful to Peter Bishop and Helen Barnes-Bulley of Varuna, the Writers' House, for reading the story at different stages and assuring me it was worthy of telling.

Thanks also to Meg Davis, Lenore McIntosh, Laura Robinson, and Ali Smith for reading early drafts, and to Peter Bate and Natalie Wagemans for listening to my readings, without protest.

Appreciation to Di Bates, Bill Condon, Sandy Fussell, and Ann Whitehead for always encouraging me and insisting that blank pages are scarier than full ones.

Thanks to Sarah Foster, Sue Whiting, and the professional team at Walker Books Australia. I am honored to be a Walker Books author.

Finally, huge thanks to my editor, Suzanne O'Sullivan. Without your belief in me and my writing, and your gentle and nurturing guidance, *Out of This Place* could not have become the story it deserved to be.